The Cumberlands of Caliente

Sheryl A. M. Seager

October 28, 2019

The Cumberlands of Caliente

This book is a work of fiction, although many events in this book transpired.

Contributors:

Deena L. Goodale

Bill and Lynnette J. Barber

Edna M. Haley Grensing

City of Caliente, Nevada

M James Lillywhite

Cambria L. Park

The Cumberlands of Caliente

In Memory of

Georgia Haley Seager

Caliente Depot

---

[1] Courtesy of City of Caliente, Nevada

Caliente Depot

---

[2] Courtesy of City of Caliente, Nevada

Caliente Depot

[3] Courtesy of City of Caliente, Nevada

⁴ *Caliente Depot*

---

⁴ Courtesy of City of Caliente, Nevada

Caliente Depot [5]

---

[5] Courtesy of Bill and Lynnette Barber

*The Roscoe Haley family on Denton Heights,
Caliente, Nevada
Circa 1935*

⁶ Company Row Caliente, Nevada

---
⁶ Courtesy of M James Lillywhite

The Cumberlands of Caliente

The Cumberlands of Caliente

Chapter one

Summer 1929

Syd Cumberland checks his pocket watch for the second time and then stuffs it back in his vest pocket. He will need to leave for his office earlier than usual today. Most Saturdays he is there by 9:00 and is gone by noon. But this Saturday the Garrets and the Whitmans need some additional accounting and bookkeeping done. And they will be bringing the paperwork to Syd early so they can get back to their businesses. The Garrets have a mercantile store that's open six days a week. Syd does all of their bookkeeping. The Whitmans own a local hotel that is always open. He manages their investments and does all of their accounting. When he officially opens at 9:00 a.m., it will be a busy day for him. There are the walk-in customers who stop by to drop off work, or others who just want to ask questions, and others who come in just to chat.

The Cumberlands of Caliente

With the company having been in Syd's family for several decades, he knows that his father and his grandfather would be proud of him for his continued success with the business. It has been profitable for the fifteen years that he's owned it.

Recently, Syd hired a competent young man to assist him, but it still isn't enough to keep up with the growing demand for his services. The business is taking so much time away from his family that he's worried it's taking a toll on them. Syd steps away from his thoughts to head to the kitchen for breakfast when he hears his wife calling him.

"Syd, your breakfast is ready. Girls, James, come to the breakfast table. We need to hurry if we want to make the early train." Belle, Syd's wife, scurries about their kitchen and then sets a hot breakfast on the table for her family. Syd loves the fresh eggs that Belle buys from their neighbor. They make wonderful omelets, and go nicely with the imported cheeses that they get on occasion. The Dutch cocoa that they order from Holland is always a special treat.

Syd is proud of his family. Belle has always been a wonderful wife to him and a good mother to their four children.

The Cumberlands of Caliente

His three beautiful daughters and handsome son are good children and a joy to him. He couldn't ask for a better family.

"Ella, hurry up and put your shoes on or we're going to miss the train. And your father needs to get to work early today too." Said Belle.

"Sorry Mama. I can't find the other shoe." Said Ella.

"Well, then get a different pair."

"They won't match my dress." Ella has a concerned look on her face and searches some more. "Oh, I found the other one."

"Hurry, your father is in the Studebaker waiting for us."

Ella runs to the front room and stands in front of her mother like a tin soldier. "Ready."

Belle guides most of her children inside their car. But Mary chooses to ride on the running board outside of the car. She loves the breeze flowing through her hair, and it's cooler than riding inside.

"James, you get to stay with Mrs. Winton today and play with her kittens."

"Yeah. I love the kitties."

Liza whispers to her mother. "Why isn't James going with us?"

"He's too little and would get too tired. We'll be shopping all day and we won't get home until late." Said Belle.

They hear the train whistle warning as they approach the station. Syd pulls to a stop at the depot. Then Mary jumps off the running board, and Belle, Ella, and Liza climb out of the car.

"Hurry girls. The train will be leaving in just a few minutes."

Belle and her daughters rush to the waiting train. She hands their tickets to the conductor; then they step aboard and quickly find seats. Soon the train pulls away from the station and heads south toward Las Vegas.

"I like watching the sagebrush out the window. It blows a lot when we pass it." Ella can't keep her eyes off of the view. "Hey Liza, look at the horses."

"They're beautiful. I'd like to ride one sometime." Said Liza.

"Mama, what all are we going to buy today?" Asks Mary

"You girls need some Sunday clothes and some school clothes. I told your father I would get him some suspenders and neckties. For me, I'd like hats for church and some dressy clothes."

"Las Vegas has bigger stores than Caliente, doesn't it Mama?" Asks Ella.

"Yes it does, we will have a lot of clothes and shoes to choose from Ella." Said Belle.

"I'd like to get some toys today." Said Liza.

"I'm sorry Liza, but we're not buying toys. We're buying clothes. And maybe I'll get my girls some chocolate, candy sticks, or other kinds of candy if you're good."

"Yeah." Comes from all three girls.

"Mama, how come we're going to Las Vegas to shop? We usually just buy out of the catalogs like we do for Christmas." Asks Mary.

"I thought it would be fun to take the train to Las Vegas, have lunch somewhere, and then shop. And it's better to try on shoes before you buy them. That way you'll know if they fit or not." Said Belle.

"I love going to Las Vegas, and I like shopping. It's fun. I was just wondering." Said Mary.

The Cumberlands of Caliente

The train's brakes hiss and the engineer blows the whistle signaling its stop at the Main Station in Las Vegas. Steam puffs from the top and enters the sky competing with the low-lying clouds. Belle wakes up Ella and Liza from their short nap. Then all four of them take the steps down to the platform and turn in the direction of the downtown area. They walk the two blocks to the center of town where most of the stores are located. Soon they see a large department store that has large glass windows and a big wood and glass front door. They look up to see a huge sign stating METGAN'S DEPARTMENT STORE & DRY GOODS.

"If you girls are hungry, we can eat in Metgans. They usually have roast beef and gravy with mashed potatoes."

Ella licks her lips. "Yum. I hope they have lots of gravy for the potatoes."

"I'm sure they do." Said Belle.

"Can we have some pie too Mama?" Asks Liza.

"We can share some. I don't think you girls need a whole piece of pie."

"Okay Mama. But I can eat a whole piece of pie." Said Liza.

"Oh I know you can, but I also know that you'll want some candy sticks or chocolates later."

"Yes, I do."

Belle and her daughters step inside the large restaurant on the main level of Metgan's Department Store. After they're seated and given menus, Belle removes her gloves. Then Mary, Ella, and Liza follow suit. Belle takes care of the ordering for all four of them. Soon steaming plates of roast beef, mashed potatoes with gravy, and buttered green beans are brought to their table served on plates made of fine bone imported china. At the end of their meal, Mary and Ella share a piece of fresh peach pie with a scoop of French vanilla ice cream. Belle and Liza share a slice of fresh strawberry rhubarb pie with whipped cream.

After lunch is over, they follow the signs to get to the escalator for their ride to the third floor where the children's department is located.

"Mama, I'm always afraid that the escalator is going to suck me in when we get to the top, or do the same thing when we get to the bottom." Said Liza.

Belle smiles to herself and then looks down to Liza. "Just hold my hand and you'll be okay."

"Thanks Mama." Liza grabs her mother's hand and doesn't let go until they reach the third floor.

A middle-aged woman in a fine tailored black suit comes over to greet them as they step off the escalator and turn toward the children's department. "Hello, what may I help you with today?"

"Madam, we need dresses, shoes, socks, slips, and underwear. Some of the dresses will need to be for church and others for school." Replies Belle.

"Right this way please. Would you like to start with the dresses first?" The sales clerk asks.

"That's fine."

"Mama, I would like some blue dresses and some green ones." Said Mary.

The sales lady looks Mary over. Then points her in the right direction. "Your size will be over in that section. And there are several racks of dresses to chose from."

"Thank you."

Mary moves toward the clothing that would fit her. She looks through several racks before stopping at one that has dresses made in more elegant fabrics. The first dress that gets her attention is one in deep green that would be for church or dressier events.

The Cumberlands of Caliente

Then she finds another dress in navy blue just for church. She switches to another rack and lifts out a deep red dress with silver buttons, and then a gray two piece dress in polished cotton with pink trim. The last two she pulled out will be for school.

"Mama, my red dresses are too small. May I get some more red ones and a pink one for church please?" Asks Ella.

"Yes of course."

The saleswoman directs Ella to a rack of dresses in varying colors. Ella pulls out a bright red dress with pearl buttons. Then she selects another dress in light pink, in a similar style for church. She lifts out a mauve colored dress that has tiny flowers all over the bodice and adds that to her first two choices. Her favorite dress is the last one she spies. It's red plaid with rows of ribbon on the bottom. It has a jacket to go with it. Then it's Liza's turn to chose.

"I don't care what colors mine are. I like all colors." Said Liza. She pulls out dresses with lots of details. One is in deep purple with ruffles on the sleeves. The next one is maroon with black satin ribbon on the bodice and hemline, and then another one is emerald green with double rows of brass buttons going down the front. Her last pick is a striped pale gold dress with tiny carved buttons.

After they're through choosing and trying on dresses, they get fitted for shoes.

"Mama, these shoes are a little big." Ella says as she wiggles her foot around inside her shoe.

"We'll just put a little paper in the toes and they'll be okay. You're growing like a weed. So they will fit perfectly in no time." Said Belle.

"May I get some shiny black shoes for church?" Asks Ella.

"Yes of course. They're called patent leather. Black is always the best color choice for fall and winter. I will get some for your sisters too."

"Oh. I'll try to remember that name." Ella says quietly to herself. "Patent leather. Patent leather."

After the girls are through with their shopping, they head to the men's department for Belle to get some suspenders and neckties for Syd. She loves the bold color choices for the men's ties. And she knows that Syd will like them too.

Their next stop is in the women's dress department for Belle to get some Sunday clothes. The first article of clothing that catches her eye is a gray-blue fine tailored suit with matching covered buttons. Her next find is a dusty rose-colored dress in silk shantung with mother of pearl buttons. She lifts one more dress out of the rack that will be for all occasions. The color is deep teal with pewter colored buttons. She knows that Syd will love the color on her.

"Mama that pink dress looked really pretty on you when you tried it on. The color is beautiful."

"Why thank you Liza."

Belle adds to her growing collection a navy blue skirt, a red floral print ruffled blouse, and a cream-colored pin tuck blouse.

Then they head to the millinery department. Belle tries on several hats before deciding on a light gray one and a cream colored one with matching trim.

The candy counter is their last stop. Mary chooses peppermint sticks, root beet sticks, and butterscotch sticks. Ella picks out jellybeans in different flavors. Liza latches onto chocolates with gooey marshmallow centers. Belle knows how much Syd likes fine chocolate so she buys some with hazel nuts and others with rich chocolate centers. To finish her candy buying, she picks out licorice and candy sticks for James.

With everything bagged and boxed up for them to carry out, Belle hires a car to take them to the train station with all of their purchases. Belle, Mary, Ella, and Liza climb in the waiting car. Then the driver loads all of their boxes, zippered bags, and sacks in the trunk and takes off toward the train station.

After the short ride, Belle pays the fare and adds a tip. The driver unloads their boxes and bags and passes them off to a porter who is standing there waiting to greet them.

"Welcome madam and young ladies. Do you want to check your shopping bags?" He looks up at Belle and then smiles to Mary, Ella, and Liza who are standing next to their mother. Ella giggles at being called a young lady.

"Yes, we need to stow these for our travel to Caliente." Said Belle.

Liza speaks up. "Be real careful with them. They are our new dresses and shoes for school and church."

"Yes, young lady, I will handle them very carefully. I wouldn't want them to get wrinkled or dirty."

Liza curtsies and then bows. "Thank you sir."

Belle grabs Liza's hand before she falls over doing her curtsy.

"Madam, here is your claim ticket. They will be unloaded with the rest of the baggage when you reach Caliente."

The Cumberlands of Caliente

"Thank you." Belle hands some coins to the porter. Then they walk toward the train steps. She hands their tickets to the conductor. Then they climb aboard the train and find seats facing each other with Ella opposite Belle. The bright afternoon sun is streaming through the windows. So Belle pulls her shade down to stop the glare. But Ella leaves hers up to watch the countryside as the train moves quickly north.

Later that evening when the train pulls into the station, Syd is standing there with James at his side. Soon Belle, Mary, Ella, and Liza step off the train and head to their waiting family members.

"Papa, come see what we bought?" Asks Liza.

"When we get home, you'll have to show me. Did you have fun today?" Asks Syd.

"We did. Our lunch was so good. And Mama bought us some sweets at the candy counter. We brought some for you and James too."

"Well, thank you. Were my girls well behaved today?"

"We all were Papa." Said Mary. Then Belle nods her head.

"I'm glad you were good. Let's go home and have some dinner." Said Syd.

"Good because I'm really hungry." Said Ella.

"We can have that chicken and rice that is leftover from last night. I made a lot on purpose. So dinner won't take long to fix. We also have plenty of fresh peaches." Said Belle.

"Do we have cream for the peaches?" Asks Liza.

"There should be some in the ice box if one of you didn't have all of it on your oatmeal." Said Belle.

"I had just a little." Said Liza.

"I had some. But I think there was still a little left when I was done." Said Ella.

Chapter two

Liza slips on one of her new dresses, twirls around in their bedroom, and then looks in the mirror. She wishes she knew how to sew beautiful dresses like this one. She loves all the intricate details that go into making it.

Mary, Ella, and Liza can't wait to wear their newly purchased clothing when they walk out the door for the new school year. They donate their outgrown clothing to some neighbors in need who live down the hill. The young girls in that family are thrilled to have clothing passed down to them. They don't care that they're second hand because they will have some really nice things to wear to school and church. And they don't mind that the shoes have been worn before.

September had been a beautiful month, but October is edging toward cooler weather. The leaves have turned color and started to fall during the last three weeks of October. Belle is in the kitchen preparing a hot meal to help ward off the cool temperatures of autumn. And Mary is at her side assisting her. Their dinner will be ham, baked potatoes, homemade bread, and a creamy custard for dessert. Belle stops what she's doing to get her second daughter's attention.

"Ella, will you run outside and get the newspaper so it will be ready for your father when he gets home?" Asks Belle.

"Okay, Mama."

Ella retrieves the paper from the porch, opens it, and walks back inside wearing a frown while staring at the printed pages.

"Mama, I know what a crash is, but what's the stock market? Is it animals like the Smithsons have?"

"Let me see what you're reading Ella." Belle's face is creased with worry as she peruses the front page and then turns the page to read some more. She thinks to herself. 'She will need to talk to Syd about this when he comes home.' "I'm not sure what this is all about Ella. But it's not about animals."

"Oh. Maybe Papa knows."

"He probably does."

Later that night, Belle speaks softly to Syd in their bedroom broaching the topic about the stock market decline that she read about in the newspaper earlier that day. "Is the stock market situation bad for us?" Asks Belle.

"Before I left work, I heard some talk from clients when they came into the business late this afternoon. So I read the paper as soon as I got home. I'm worried Belle. A lot of our money was invested in the stock market. It doesn't look good. Maybe the market will turn around in a few days or even a few weeks. But I doubt it. I hope that I can keep the business a float. Some of my clients might not be able to hire me anymore or even pay me what they owe if they begin to have financial woes. I'm sure we're not the only ones affected with what happened to the stock market today. We might have to cut corners in some areas if the market doesn't improve really soon."

"What do you mean Syd?"

"We'll probably have to spend a lot less on Christmas this year, and on some of the nice foods and things that we always enjoy."

"Do you really think it's that serious?"

"Yes. I do. I hope that I'm not jumping to conclusions, but the stock market dropped thirty points today. That's the most that

I've ever seen it do. So I'll be keeping a close eye on it to see if anything changes."

"Oh Syd!" Belle says nervously as she covers her mouth with her hand.

During the following weeks, Syd reviews daily the stock market trend. The stock prices are still near the bottom with the companies where he was so heavily invested. The market values have come to a standstill and haven't moved up in weeks.

Chapter three

Three months later

Syd is feeling dejected and has a look on his face portraying it when he enters his home later than usual after a long workweek. He tries to put on a brave face in front of his family while they are at the dinner table. But he's not fooling Belle. After their dinner is over and the dishes are done, she confronts him in the parlor while he's reading the paper.

"What is going on Syd? How bad are things for us?"

Syd folds up the newspaper. "I can't break it to you gently. It's terrible for us. I'm glad that we inherited our house, so it's paid for. The money that I put in the stock market is gone, all of it. There are several clients that can't pay me either. And others have pulled out because they can't afford my services anymore. I still have a few clients left, but I had to let my assistant go."

Syd takes a deep breath before continuing. "I shouldn't have put off the repairs that needed to be done on our house. I thought to myself. 'Ah, the roof will be fine until summer.' And concerning the other repairs that needed to be done inside our house, I kept thinking. 'I'll hire someone and have those done before Christmas.' I shouldn't have done that. I checked our roof last weekend when I noticed a leak in one if the upstairs rooms that was brought on by the recent rainstorm. The roof really needs to be fixed now. I'm so sorry Belle."

Belle covers her face and starts crying. Syd wraps his arm around her and gives her a hug to help comfort her.

"What are we going to do Syd?"

"I don't know yet. I'm still working on it. Many people are optimistic, but I think it could take our country a long time to recover from this fiasco. And another thing. I'm not sure how long my business will survive if everybody around us is having financial trouble. I can't afford to lose any more clients. But we'll figure something out. We'll survive, somehow." Said Syd.

After scrimping on food, using up what savings they had, cutting corners as much as possible, and charging his remaining clients much less, Syd is forced to close his doors four months later. Many of his customers were not able to pay him what they owe because their businesses were not doing well. The remaining clients' business and payments have dwindled to almost nothing. Syd is saddened that this had to be done. He partnered with his father many years ago. His father had partnered with Syd's grandfather who had started the business. The company had been in his family for several decades and three generations. Now it's no longer an operating entity.

Syd hates seeing his family suffer because of his bad investments and business failure. Their home needs repairs done inside and out. A new roof or repairs to it is the first thing that needs to happen. Syd realized that some time ago but didn't take action. Some of their furniture is breaking down. He had planned to buy some new furniture pieces the previous Christmas. But with money being so tight, it didn't happen. And his family still needs to eat, and have clothes and shoes to wear. While Syd is running these thoughts around in his mind, he overhears his middle daughter talking to her mother about her needs.

"Mama, my shoes are too tight." Exclaims Ella.

"Well, take the paper out that I stuffed in them."

The Cumberlands of Caliente

"I already did that Mama."

"I will see if I can get you another pair. What about your other shoes?"

"They're all too small and hurt my feet."

"Okay. I'll try to get some more shoes for you."

The next day Belle hands over a pair of shoes to Ella. "Here, try these."

Ella looks them over. "These are old and I think that someone wore them a while. Mama you should probably take them back to the store and get another pair."

"Ella, I didn't get them at a store. Our neighbor Mrs. Farley gave them to me. Her daughter couldn't wear them anymore because they were too small for her."

Ella starts to cry. "I don't want to wear somebody else's old shoes."

"I'm sorry. That's all I have right now Ella."

Ella wipes her eyes with the back of her hand. "That's okay. I'm sorry Mama. I really am. I know that you and Papa are doing the best that you can. I will just polish them, buff them, and they will look just like new. Thank you."

The Cumberlands of Caliente

A few minutes later Syd walks in the door looking tired and dejected after finishing the first week at his new job working for the railroad. He notices that Ella had been crying.

"How was your day dear?" Belle asks while trying to be upbeat.

"It's a lot of physical labor that I'm not used to doing. I'm sure it will get better in time. I'm glad that I've got this job though." Said Syd.

"Me too. I hope things will get better soon. Your newspaper is in the parlor, and dinner is just about ready."

"Thank you Belle."

"We have biscuits and gravy. And we have a few green onions from our early garden. So we can have some green onions to go with our bread and milk. And Mrs. Farley had a few apples that she stored that were from her apple tree. So she shared some with us, and I made apple turnovers. I gave her some dresses that Liza had outgrown since we don't have another daughter to pass them down to."

"Thank you dear. I'm glad that we can help each other out." Syd starts rubbing his hands together in a nervous fashion.

"Belle, I need to talk to you about something after the kids are in bed."

Belle gets a worried look on her face. "You're not losing your job are you?"

"No, it's fine. They like my work very much. It's about something else."

Later that evening Syd sits down with Belle in their parlor and explains the situation that he brought up before dinner. "Belle, the superintendent at the railroad called me over to talk just before I left work today. He told me that he'd like to buy some of our furniture if there's anything that we'd like to sell. He knows that we have some really nice pieces. We wouldn't get nearly what we paid for them. But is there anything that you'd be willing to part with?" Syd asks nervously.

Belle thinks for a moment, and then takes a deep breath before answering. "Syd, maybe we should sell the pieces that would bring us the most money. You bought me that beautiful deep violet davenport that's in our parlor for an anniversary present. I'd hate to see it go. But we need shoes and clothes for some of our children. And our roof and house need some repairs done too."

Syd looks down and then back up at Belle. "Are there any other pieces of furniture that you'd be willing to sell?"

"Maybe we should sell our bed and move the one from the spare room to our room. We also have that large overstuffed chair in the parlor that matches our davenport. It's very nice and it's practically brand new. So that might be another good choice. We could move some pieces of furniture from other rooms to the parlor to have enough seating. The spare room has a little. And there might be some in the attic."

"That should help us for a while, and we could get the repairs that need to be done on the inside and outside of our house. I'm sure our children could use some new shoes. They are growing like weeds." Said Syd.

"They are. I will look in the catalog for shoes for James and for the girls. I could probably find some for a good value. Prices in the recent catalogs seemed to have dropped quite a bit."

"It's probably because of the state of affairs in our country. People can't pay what they used to pay for things. And luxury items are only for the rich." Said Syd.

Three days later, two men jump out of a truck and head for the Cumberland family's front door. Belle opens the door when

The Cumberlands of Caliente

she sees them coming up the walk. "Mrs. Cumberland, we've come to pick up some furniture that your husband sold to the superintendent at the railroad."

"I will show you where the furniture is. Please come this way." The men follow Belle to the parlor. She points out her luxurious davenport and matching overstuffed chair. And then they head with her to the upstairs bedrooms of her house. They come down the stairs carrying the master bed and take it out to the truck. Then they come back to pick up the davenport and chair.

Belle eyes are tearing up when she sees them load her precious davenport and other pieces of their furniture into the truck and take off. She will miss the beautiful davenport that her husband bought her for a present just two years ago. But her family needs food and clothing more than those pieces of furniture.

Chapter four

When the warmest days of summer arrive, the financial situation hasn't improved much for the Cumberland family. Even though Syd is working long hours, the pay is much lower than what he'd been making at his own business before the stock market crash. And he isn't able to set money aside like he'd done in the past. At least their home and roof are in better shape than they were just a few months ago. The leaks have stopped, and the walls don't have outside air breathing in through them.

"Mama, do we get to go to Las Vegas again and shop for school clothes and Sunday clothes? We really had a lot of fun, and the food we ate at Metgan's was so good. So was the candy." Asks Liza.

"No, Liza we can't afford it. I can make you some candy, but we can't buy any clothes from Las Vegas like we did last year."

"Oh, I'll tell Ella we can't 'ford it. She was talking to me about it this morning."

"But there is a store on Front Street where we can go."

"The only one I remember on Front Street said 'Thrift Shop.' Is that it?"

"Yes, that's it Liza."

"What's a thrift shop Mama?"

"It's a store where people give their things that they can't use anymore. Then other people can shop for clothes, shoes, furniture, toys, and other things."

"So we'd get to buy things that other people don't want?" Liza wrinkles her face into a frown as she says it.

"Well, I guess you could say that. I do have another idea Liza. I could sew some clothes for you and your sisters."

"I think that I would like that much better. Where do you get things to sew clothes?"

The Cumberlands of Caliente

"There's a store on Clover Street that has cloth, patterns, buttons, zippers, thread, and pretty trims for dresses and other types of clothing."

"Oh I'd like that. Could we go there tomorrow?"

"I will talk to your father about it tonight. If he says yes, we would still have to wait until he gets paid on Friday. Maybe we could go on Saturday if it's okay with him."

"Really Mama?"

"Maybe. But remember, I still need to talk to your father about it first. Okay?"

"Yeah!"

With cash in her pocketbook, Belle takes Mary, Ella and Liza with her for a walk to town to buy fabric and notions to make dresses for them.

"Now girls, you can each choose cloth for two dresses. Don't pick out anything that's more than twenty-nine cents a yard. While you're picking material, I'll find some patterns and let you choose which ones you like."

The Cumberlands of Caliente

Liza looks straight ahead and runs to a fabric that catches her attention. She pulls part of it out to show her mother. "Mama, I like this color. What's it called?"

"I would call it maroon."

"I really, really like it and it's only nineteen cents a yard."

"That's very good Liza. Now, go pick another one."

Liza runs to some more fabrics that catch her interest. "Mama, I found this one and I found this one that are really pretty." Liza points to them. "But I can't make up my mind."

"Why don't you hold them both up?"

Liza pulls a little of each one out and tries to put them in front of her face.

"Let's carry them to the cutting table. That way you can spread them out and see the designs on each fabric a little better." Said Belle.

She helps Liza lift out the heavy bolts of fabric and lay them out on the table. Then she looks at both bolts. "Liza, I think that you would look better in the blue-green color. The brown fabric doesn't look quite as good on you because the print is a little big. But the blue-green one has a small print and contrasts nicely with your golden brown hair and eyes."

"You know Mama, I think that I like the blue and green one better anyway. The design is prettier because of the little hearts on it." Liza checks the price on top of the bolt and slumps down. "Oh, Mama, I didn't look at the price. It's thirty-five cents a yard."

"That's okay. Your other one was only nineteen cents a yard. Let's see what your sisters have found." Belle walks toward Mary and Ella. "What did you find Mary?"

"I like this blue one. It's like the color of the sky with no clouds. And I found this other one that reminds me of a seashell that I saw in a book one time."

"Mary, that color is called coral. You'd look good in that color. It goes well with your dark hair. In fact, both of those colors look really good on you."

Belle turns to her other daughter. "Show me what you picked Ella."

"I like this red one and this red one. Which one do you like best Mama?"

Belle looks them over. "I like them both. The prints on each one are quite different. They would both go well with your golden blond hair. Do you want two red dresses Ella?"

"Yes. I think I do."

Belle steps away to the pattern counter and looks through the books for a few minutes. Then she pulls several patterns from the cabinet and softly closes the metal drawers behind her. She returns to her daughters with her arm full of patterns.

"Okay, girls, I will show you the patterns that I picked. You can each choose one. Each pattern has three different ways to make it."

They each pick their favorite from the stack, and then choose some buttons and trims for their dresses.

Before finishing their shopping, Belle pulls some zippers and matching thread from the racks. Then she adds some elastic to her pile to use on the sleeves of some of the dresses.

"Since you were all so well behaved today, and we finished so quickly, we can stop at the drug store and get an ice cream cone. We'll take some Fudgesicles home for your father and James."

"Yeah." Yells Liza and Ella.

"Thanks Mama." Comes from Mary.

"Let's get going so that we don't have to leave James too long with Mrs. Winton." Said Belle.

The Cumberlands of Caliente

"Mama, do you suppose we could get some new socks? You mended mine, but they have new holes in them." Asks Mary.

"Yes, I will get socks for all of you. We'll stop at the five and dime before we get our ice cream. They should have some in stock in your sizes. James could use some new ones too. And your father needs some new work socks. You girls just pick white ones."

"Mama, white is so boring." Said Mary.

"But Mary, white goes with everything and they would look nice for church too."

Mary sighs. "Okay Mama. I guess they do."

Belle and her daughters cross the railroad tracks to get to the five and dime store across the street. When they walk in, Mary hurries to the back of the store where paints, brushes, and drawing paper are located. After looking at the prices on the art supplies, she quickly leaves the area with a disheartened look on her face. She wishes she could have some of them. But they can't afford it. After she finds her socks, she goes looking for her mother and sisters.

Ella holds up some socks. "Mama, I found these red socks. They are not white like you said we should get, but they are only five cents."

"That's fine. You can get those because your new dresses will be red."

"Thanks Mama."

"Liza and Mary, have you found any socks?"

"Yes, Mama." Said Mary.

"I need helping picking out mine. I don't know what size I wear. But I saw some white ones with pretty lace that I like." Smiles Liza.

"I will help you." Belle looks at the price of the socks with lace and sighs. But she decides to buy them anyway.

"When do we get to wear our new dresses?" Asks Liza.

"I will start sewing them on Monday."

Then Belle points to each of her daughters. "If all three of you help around the house and do some of the cooking, maybe I can have your dresses made by the end of the next week or the week after."

"I'll help a lot." Said Ella.

"Me too." Said Liza. "But I'm not sure how much I can cook."

"But you know how to clean Liza. You can sweep the floor, set the table, and help with the dishes."

"Yes, I can do that." She smiles.

"I will still need to wash the clothes. But Ella, maybe you can help hang them on the line. And Mary, if we have any butter, would you make some cookies? Your father likes to take them for his lunch. And all of us like to eat cookies and fruit for dessert with our dinner."

"I love to make cookies Mama. And I especially like to eat them." Laughs Mary.

"Don't we all? Oh, and, Mrs. Granger gave me some brisket because she had a lot. So we can have stew for our Sunday dinner tomorrow. That will be a special treat for us. I found a special on potatoes. So I kept some for us and gave some to Mrs. Granger. We try to help each other. That's what being neighborly is all about."

"I think that we are good neighbors, don't you Mama?" Asks Mary.

"I sure hope we are."

The Cumberlands of Caliente

With her three daughters helping around the house with everyday chores, doing some of the cooking, and beating the rugs outside to get the dust and dirt out, Belle is able to complete the sewing projects, and get the dresses made before the school year starts.

Mary, with the help of her mother, learned how to sew the buttons on one of her dresses. Liza is fascinated with the details that go into making clothes. She watched her mother throughout much of the sewing process.

At the end of her first week of school, Ella excitedly rushes in the door, drops her books on the piano bench, and goes looking for her mother.

"Mama, these dresses are much prettier than what we bought in Las Vegas last year. The girls at school really liked them and wanted to know where we bought them. I told them proudly that my mother made them for me. Thank you Mama for making us such beautiful dresses." Ella twirls in front of her mother and then curtsies.

The Cumberlands of Caliente

Belle has tears in her eyes when she hears her daughter speak so highly of her. "Why thank you Ella. I appreciate what you said. I'm glad you really like them."

Liza joins in. "I love mine too Mama. I hope that you can sew us dresses again. I would like one for Christmas that has rows and rows of ribbons on it, some pretty lace, and shiny buttons."

"Thank you Liza. I hope that we can afford it. You like other things for Christmas too."

"Yes, I do. But dresses are my favorite things to get."

Mary overhears the conversation and enters the room to join in. "I like the fabric that I picked for my dresses. It moves when I walk. And the cloth is so soft. Thanks Mama for making them for me."

"I'm glad that you like your new dresses. It was fun making them for all of you. Now, will the three of you help me get dinner on the table so it will be on time when your father comes home?" Then Belle smiles at them. "And we'd all better hurry."

Three sets of busy hands help their mother with the dinner preparations. Soon a lovely meal is laid out for the family. There is butter to put on the baked potatoes. The seasoned roasted chicken smells heavenly with the herbs that came from their kitchen herb garden. The peas from their outdoor garden are sweet and tender. To top off the meal they have a berry pie made from fresh, in season blueberries.

Chapter five

Three years later

The sudden howling of the wind, that's rattling the windows, gets Belle's attention. She wraps her sweater around herself tightly; then she looks out the window and watches as the leaves blow off the trees. Their big house is hard to keep warm even in the fall. Tonight's supper will be without meat again. The chickens that they bought last year are gone, so their eggs are too. Tonight they will feast on vegetable stew and biscuits. Their bountiful summer garden has been a blessing. It has given them a variety of vegetables to choose from. Luckily their root cellar keeps them from going bad.

Belle grabs her coat before going outside to check their coal supply. She lifts the lid and looks in the bin; it's getting really low. Again. She will have to let Syd know when he gets home. Belle turns around, steps in the house, and goes looking for Ella.

"Ella, you need to practice the piano today."

"Ah, Mama, do I have to?"

"Yes, you do. We're lucky we didn't have to sell our piano."

"Okay, but I need a glass of cold water first. My throat hurts."

"I hope you're not getting sick."

"I don't think so. I'm just really, really thirsty. I think it's because of something salty that I ate. My school friend gave me some salt rock and I licked it a few times."

"Yes, it is salty. And Ella, they give it to animals."

"Yuck, I didn't know that Mama."

"It's true."

"I won't be licking that anymore."

"Ella, there should be some cold water in the icebox, but don't drink it all. Leave some for your father because he likes it cold just like you do. Then come back and practice, practice, practice."

"Yes, Mama."

As the afternoon comes to a close, Belle finds Mary in the girls' bedroom with her sketchpad, drawing trees and a lake. There are several other sketches lying around the bedroom displaying other outdoor settings. Belle puts the clean laundry on each of the girls' beds; then stops to look at Mary's drawings.

"Mary, your sketches are really good. May I see your paintings too?"

"Sure, let me get them. I wish that I had more colors. What I'd like for Christmas are more paints, paper, canvases, and maybe some new brushes. All I want to do is paint. When I finish this drawing I hope to paint a picture that looks like my drawing. Maybe on Saturday I can do that."

"After your chores are done on Saturday, you can use the rest of the afternoon to paint."

"Really? Before it gets dark tonight is it okay if I take my chalk and draw on the rocks behind the house?"

"Yes, of course, but be sure that you put your sweater and coat on. It's cold out there." Then Belle smiles to Mary. "Those old ugly rocks will look a whole lot prettier when you're done with them."

"Thank you Mama."

After Mary grabs her coat and chalk, she runs out the door. Then Belle goes looking for Liza to help her with her new sewing project. She finds her in the attic room with her fabric and a pattern laid out on a small table. Liza is puzzling over what she should do next.

"That flour sack fabric will sure make a pretty apron Liza. Do you need help with it?"

"I think that I figured it out Mama. But could you check the way that I pinned the pattern before I start cutting?"

Belle looks at the fabric layout that Liza is working on.

"It's unusual the way that you did it. But it will be very pretty made that way."

"I wanted my apron to be different. So I angled it to have the flowers going down in rows on the fabric."

"That is what's called 'on the bias.' It's a diagonal layout. I like the way that you think Liza. It makes your clothing stand out from others."

"I'd like to put three pieces of trim on an angle too. Uh, I mean the bias."

"I have lots of trims for you to choose from Liza. I took some trims that were still good off of some old dresses and other things. There might be some pretty trims that were on some pillows that wore out. And I might have some fringe, ric rac, braiding, and maybe some ribbon in my sewing basket."

"Really? When you have time Mama, I'd like to lay the trims on my apron fabric. I love sewing. Maybe I can design really beautiful dresses someday." Dreams Liza.

"Maybe you can dear." And Belle thinks to herself. 'Maybe she can.'

The Cumberlands of Caliente

Chapter six

Two years later

Belle tosses and turns most nights while trying to fall asleep. She's worried that they won't be able to take care of their growing family. At least Syd has a job, even though his raises have been small.

It's sad that many of their neighbors have husbands who are out of work. This depression is eating on her. Will things get better anytime soon? How are people doing in the rest of the country? Are many of them out of work and hungry?

Some days she wakes up just as tired as when she went to bed the night before. Her brain can't seem to slow down. What if Syd gets sick? What will they do if one of their children gets really sick?

Belle quits worrying for a while and goes about her day-to-day chores. Later that afternoon while she's working on dinner preparations, she hears Syd come in and call out to her. He has a huge smile on his face when he comes in the kitchen looking for her. Some days those smiles are few and far between.

"Belle, I just found out today that I'm being promoted to supervisor. So I'll be getting a raise." He pauses for a moment. "But I will be putting in more hours too."

"That's wonderful Dear. I hate to have you gone more. But we still need to feed and clothe our family, and keep our home in good repair." Belle starts stirring something on the stove before continuing.

"Syd, I know that you've done a good job fixing our dining room chairs, but soon we'll need to get some more. The wood is starting to splinter. I don't know if you noticed, but our bed sheets are wearing out too. I doubt that the second hand store would have any. Most people wear out their sheets instead of donating them to charity." Belle stops stirring and looks at Syd. "I'm sorry Syd; I shouldn't be burdening you with all of this. You don't need it right now."

"That's okay dear. When the new catalog comes, maybe there will be some sheets in it that are affordable. Mr. Maynard is a carpenter, and he's looking for work. I could ask him to make two chairs at a time. In six weeks we could have six new chairs."

"That would be wonderful, thanks Syd. I'll see what I can find in the catalog for our bed. And I hope you can work out a deal with Mr. Maynard." Said Belle.

After church the following Sunday, Mary and Ella help their mother put a hot meal on the table to celebrate Syd's raise and promotion. Belle can't remember the last time that they had a really good pot roast with gravy, or a cup of delicious hot cocoa. All three girls take care of the cleanup. James is in the front room reading a book when he sees his parents walk hand in hand out the door for a Sunday afternoon stroll.

"Belle, getting that thirty-five dollars a month raise has really helped us. I can get the materials that I need to do other repairs around the house that have come up recently. And it will help pay for having new dining room chairs made. Mr. Maynard is happy for the extra work. He said that making those chairs will be his evening income."

The Cumberlands of Caliente

"Things seem to be looking up for us Syd. I told you about Mary doing some babysitting for the Stephens' family. She's getting paid in canvases and paints. Margie Stephens used to be an artist in Las Vegas doing work for some hotels until she got married."

"Belle, I didn't know that she was an artist."

"She was for many years. She had some extra canvases that she gave Mary because she didn't know when she'd ever get back to painting. She's been taking in mending and ironing to help support the family. And her kids keep her pretty busy too. She also gave Mary some paints because they might get too old if she kept them any longer. Mary wanted to do something in return for the paints and canvases. And Margie needed a babysitter so she could work. So Mary volunteered. It's worked out great for both of them."

"That's wonderful of our Mary to do that. How's Ella's piano playing going?"

"I forgot to tell you that she has a recital at the school in Panaca next Saturday evening. Her teacher, Miss Frye, said that Ella is her best student. I've been doing Miss Frye's ironing to pay for Ella's lessons. So it's a good exchange." Said Belle.

The Cumberlands of Caliente

"Belle, Liza showed me her drawings the other night. She told me she wants to design clothes when she grows up. She's really ambitious." Said Syd.

"I know. Every day she just pours through the Sears and Roebuck catalog and the Montgomery Ward one looking at the clothing. She's not too interested in the chickens that they have for sale or the farm equipment." Laughs Belle.

"I can't imagine she would be. I hope that the economy will get better soon. I know when Mary graduates from high school that she would like to go to a school that teaches art."

"Syd, it can't stay this way forever. You just got a generous raise. Mrs. Stephens told me that her husband got a raise too."

"It still could be a long time before the economic situation turns around."

"You really think so?"

"I do. There are still too many people out of work in this country."

"I guess that I didn't think that far outside of our little community." Said Belle.

"Looks like our stroll brought us back to our house. Do you want to walk some more?" Asks Syd

"Maybe just a little longer. I like spending time with you."

When Saturday evening comes, Syd and Belle load their children into their car for the ride to Panaca for Ella's piano recital. She is already there with her teacher when they walk in. After several students have played, it's Ella's turn. She has a confident smile on her face when she begins, and after she's finished. The Cumberland family clusters around her afterwards offering praise, while eating refreshments of molasses cookies and lemonade.

"You were wonderful." Mary says as she hugs Ella.

"I liked your music." Said Liza.

"Thank you." Ella rejoins the other musicians to congratulate them on their performances.

"I can't believe how beautifully Ella played. Miss Frye told me that she had a friend sitting in the audience tonight who has a music school in Las Vegas. She would like to talk to us sometime next week about Ella. It will probably be one evening after dinner when she's through teaching piano for the day." Said Belle.

"That's got me curious Belle. I wonder what she could want. Maybe she can stop by on Wednesday. I'll be off a little early that night. Could you mention that to her?"

"I will try to talk to her on Monday before you get home."

Wednesday evening after Belle and her daughters finish cleaning up supper and start putting things away, she hears a knock on their front door.

Belle calls out. "Syd that might be Miss Frye. After I talked to her on Monday, she said she would be coming over this evening."

Syd sees Miss Frye through the glass and opens the door. "Hi. Come in. My wife is just finishing up in the kitchen." Syd peeks around the corner and then back to Miss Frye. "I see her coming now. Will you join us in the parlor?"

"Yes, thank you." When Syd, Belle and Miss Frye enter the parlor, there is a plate of butter cookies waiting for them that Ella had made.

"Have a seat please?" Asks Syd.

"Thank you." Miss Frye sits down, adjusts her glasses, puts her hands in her lap, and then faces Belle and Syd. "Mr. and

The Cumberlands of Caliente

Mrs. Cumberland I want to talk to you about Ella. My friend Bert lives in Las Vegas and has a music school there. He was at the piano recital last Saturday night in Panaca. After the recital was over, he came over and spoke with me. He told me that Ella is a gifted and an exceptionally talented piano player for her age. If you could arrange it, he would like to teach her more than what I'm able to do. And he would like to do it in Las Vegas during the summer months."

"I don't know how we could afford it right now. All we'd be able to pay would be the train fare. And that's it." Said Belle.

"I have another idea. My sister lives in Las Vegas. She would love the company of a child. Would that work for both of you? And the music school would only be for two months during the summer."

"We still couldn't afford the lessons." Said Belle.

"There might be a possibility of a scholarship. There are three available for the summer. Bert has a colleague that does that for gifted students. And it is dependent upon Bert's recommendation."

"My wife and I will talk it over and get back with you."

Miss Frye quickly gets up from her chair and looks directly at Syd and Belle. "Thank you for your time Mr. and Mrs. Cumberland."

"Thank you for stopping by. I'll walk you to the door." Belle softly closes the door behind Miss Frye and turns back to Syd. "What do you think?"

"It's a lot to digest right now. I'm sure that Ella would be excited to go. But I think that she is kind of young to be living in a big city away from us for even two months." Said Syd

"We will have to think about it some more, talk with Ella, and then get back with Miss Frye." Said Belle.

The Cumberlands of Caliente

Chapter seven

Four months later

On a warm June morning, shortly after the sun had come over the hills behind their house, Belle helps Ella move her things to the front door so that Syd can load them in the family car. Belle knows that it will be a long two months while Ella is in Las Vegas attending a music school. She will miss her young daughter and hopes that she will be okay without her mother.

Belle reaches down and hugs her other three children left behind. "You mind Mary. I will be back later tonight."

"Bye Ella. I will miss you. Said Liza.

"You have fun in Las Vegas and enjoy your music lessons." Said Mary.

"Bye Ella." Says James sadly.

After Ella's things are put in the trunk, they take off for the train station. When Syd pulls into the depot, he climbs out, unloads Ella's suitcase and satchel, and puts them on the platform. Belle carries their lunch bags from the car and hands one to Ella.

"Ella, you study hard and listen to your teacher while you're there." Said Syd.

"I will Papa." Ella reaches up, gives her father a hug, and a kiss on the cheek. Then she turns and wipes a tear from her eye before turning back.

Soon Belle and Ella hand over their tickets and climb aboard the train heading south toward Las Vegas. Ella has her face glued to the window while watching the scenery as the train speeds through the countryside. "Mama, I'm so excited to go to the music school. But I will miss you and the rest of our family." She says sadly.

Belle eyes tear up. "I will miss you too Ella. But I hope you enjoy the school and learn a lot."

"Me too."

Just before noon, Belle and Ella arrive at the Main Station in Las Vegas. Miss Frye's sister is there waiting for them. She recognizes them from the description that her sister in Caliente gave her. "Hello, I'm Grace Frye. You must be Belle and Ella."

"Yes. Nice to meet you." Belle notices Grace's quirky, but fun attire. She's wearing a bright yellow hat and has on an emerald green skirt with large white polka dots scattered all over it. Her blouse is as bright as her hat and compliments her flaming red hair.

"I can take you by the music school, but I'm sure you'd like something to eat first."

"Yes, we are a bit hungry."

"There's a small café close by, my treat." Said Grace.

"Are you sure? We can pay for lunch."

"No I'd love to do it. They have really good soups, sandwiches, and a variety of ice cream flavors. I bet Ella would like some ice cream."

"I love ice cream. But sometimes I eat too much and get sick." Laughs Ella.

"That she does. Thank you Grace." Said Belle.

"You're welcome. My car is right over there." Grace points toward it.

Belle looks in the direction that Grace is pointing and is in awe seeing a fashionable Bentley parked nearby. Could that be Grace's car? Belle asks herself.

"Don't mind my car. I got it from a friend for a song. He couldn't keep it anymore. And I needed something to drive."

When lunch is over, they take a tour of the music school. Ella strokes her hands over a large beautiful Steinway that's sitting in the middle of a performance room. A short time later, the three of them leave the school for Belle to get back to the train station.

"Thanks Grace for letting Ella stay with you."

"Yes, thank you for having me as your guest." Said Ella.

"You are both welcome. Ella and I will have a lot of fun when she's not studying. But I will make sure that she does."

"Thank you again."

Late in the afternoon, Belle kisses Ella goodbye and climbs on the train to get back to Caliente. Luckily she still has the two lunches that she and Ella didn't eat. It's way past dinnertime and she's hungry. Discreetly, she quickly eats both lunches and throws the bags in a trashcan hidden nearby.

Syd is waiting at the depot in the twilight when she arrives. After she steps off the train and onto the platform, he throws his arms around her for a hug. "Do you think that Ella will be okay for the summer?" Asks Syd.

The Cumberlands of Caliente

"I hope so. She seemed okay when I left."

Syd and Belle climb in their car for the short ride home. When they step inside their house, their girls are involved with reading and other activities. Syd walks in the parlor to pick up his unfinished book. And Belle walks in the kitchen to close the window for the night and check on her herb garden. She notices that James is sitting there by himself, having a glass of milk, and staring at the floor.

"James, is something bothering you?"

"Mama, I don't have any brothers to do things with. My sisters are always busy doing things with each other or their friends. Would you do something with me? Just you and me."

"Of course James. I'm sorry you were ignored. What would you like to do?"

"Well, since Papa is always so busy working, I was wondering if you'd like to go fishing with me?"

"I would love to go fishing with you. I used to do it with my father when I was young."

"Really?"

"Yes. I didn't have any brothers. But I was kind of a tomboy anyway, so my dad would take me fishing. Would you like to do that on Monday? We have some fishing poles in the storage shed we could use. Hopefully there are some worms in the garden that we could dig up."

"I'd like that Mama. That would be fun."

"I can pack us a lunch. But we would need to find a creek close-by because your father takes the car to work. And I don't drive anyway. There should be a creek with good fishing not too far from where we live.

"I can't wait." The sad look that was on James's face has been replaced with a smile.

"We could leave right after breakfast on Monday."

James is up and dressed while it's still dark. He quietly waits in the front room for his mother and for the others to rise. Syd is the first to walk in, and he stops to talk to James.

"It looks like your ready to go fishing James?"

He smiles. "I am. I hope we have breakfast soon so that Mama and I can leave."

"I can drop both of you off on my way to work, but you'll have to walk home."

"What about our worms?"

"Maybe you should dig some up right now before breakfast. I can help you."

James gets an even bigger smile on his face. "Would you, Papa?"

"I would love to. I'm not sure your mother likes touching worms much anyway."

"Let's go now. Maybe we can dig up the worms while it's still dark before they can run away from us."

"That's a great idea son. I'll find us a can to put them in." Syd digs through their soggy garbage, pulls out a can, and rinses it out in the sink before handing it to James. "Here you go."

"Thanks Papa."

After breakfast is eaten, Belle leaves her daughters to do the cleanup. She and James climb in the family car while Syd stows their fishing poles, bucket, and covered can of worms in the trunk. Belle has their picnic lunch and an old blanket on the back seat next to James. Soon they are off down the hill toward the nearest fishing spot.

When Syd finds a good place to fish at nearby Clover Creek, he stops the car and gets their things out of the trunk.

"James, it looks like a couple of your worms escaped. Why don't you hold the can while I put them back in?"

James sticks out his can and starts to laugh. "I guess those worms didn't want to get eaten by the fish."

His father smiles at him. "Probably not. Now you mind your mother. Don't go jumping in near the quicksand."

"I'll mind Mama, and I'll stay away from the quicksand. I don't want to be sucked under and drown."

"That probably won't happen, but do mind your mother.

After Syd leaves for work, Belle and James walk closer to the creek. She points out a large rock to him. "Do you want to sit there James? I bet we could find a few fish right below us that might want to bite. Could you put the worms on our hooks?"

James laughs. "Yeah, Papa said you don't like worms too much. I can do it."

"Thank you. Just let me know when you get hungry and I'll spread our lunch on the blanket over there."

"Okay. Mama, I see several fish down there."

"We need to be really quiet then."

"Okay." He whispers.

"I see some too." Said Belle.

The Cumberlands of Caliente

James sits with one hand on his knee and the other hand holding tightly to the pole. All of a sudden he feels a pull.

"Mama, I think that I got a fish." He yells.

"Take both your hands and pull up on the pole to hook the fish. Then pull it in."

"Look Mama, it's big one." James smiles.

"I'll grab the bucket. Maybe we'll get enough to have some for our dinner tonight."

"Oh, that would be so good. I can't wait."

By early afternoon, Belle and James have eaten their lunch of egg salad sandwiches, fruit, and cookies. They've caught enough fish to feed their family a generous trout dinner. James is already asking to go fishing again.

"Mama, I want to do this again next week."

"We can go again. But we'll have to wait a while. I promise that we will do it a few more times before summer is out."

"Promise?"

"Yes. I promise. And we need to leave some fish for other boys to catch."

"Yeah, I guess we do." Says James glumly.

The Cumberlands of Caliente

They trek from Clover Creek, cross the street, and then over the railroad tracks toward their home upon the hill.

As June days turn into July, Ella writes home that she and Grace have fun doing things together, but she misses her family. She's learning a lot, but her teacher is a strict taskmaster.

After her time at the music school draws to a close, she takes the train back to Caliente. Her family is waiting for her at the depot when she returns. As she steps off the train, she looks around and feels a little more grown up.

"Ella, I missed you. I didn't have you to play with." Said Liza.

"I missed your snoring at night." Said Mary.

"Ella, I'll grab your bags." Said Syd.

"We've all missed you." Said Belle.

"I missed you too." Said James.

Chapter eight

With Ella home from summer school, the family prepares for the upcoming school year. They get school supplies and books, and then get outfitted with new shoes.

One afternoon after playing kick the can in the street with her friends, Liza heads inside the house to look for her mother. She smiles when she finds her in the kitchen baking snicker doodle cookies. She grabs one off the table that is fresh out of the oven and has started to cool. She bites into it immediately.

"Hmm, these are so good." Liza chews some more. Mama, I was wondering if you could you sew us some dresses again for school this year? I really liked the ones you made last year." Said Liza.

"I'd love to do that for you girls. Maybe next week we can go to the mercantile store and find some material. There should be some new cloth and patterns to chose from too." Said Belle.

The Cumberlands of Caliente

"I want to help make mine this time." Said Liza.

Ella overhears the conversation going on in the kitchen and joins in.

"Mama, I really need a black dress or a dark blue one. I have to wear something like that when I play at piano recitals. Please Mama." Asks Ella.

"The mercantile store should have both of those colors with plenty of prints to choose from. Maybe we can find some cloth with dots on it. That would look really nice for a piano recital."

"Mama, do you suppose that they might have some cloth with lots of colors and maybe swirly patterns like some of the French artists' paintings?" Pipes Mary up before picking up a cookie to munch on.

"Well, I don't know if they would have anything quite like that, but maybe something close." Said Belle.

Liza, Mary, and Ella jump out of bed early on the day of their expected shopping trip. They hurry into the kitchen to fix breakfast for their mother, father, and James. They are excited for their trip to the large mercantile store in the center of town. Soon their parents and James join them in the kitchen.

The Cumberlands of Caliente

"You girls made a delicious breakfast." Said Syd.

"Yes, it is. What did you put in the eggs?" Asks Belle.

Mary pipes up. "We wanted to make the eggs a little different. So we looked in the cupboard and found some curry powder, salt, pepper, and cinnamon."

"Yes, the eggs are a little different." Smiles Belle.

"I think next time that we'll put a little less curry powder in them." Smirks Mary.

"We should probably leave out the cinnamon too." Said Ella as she scrunches up her face.

"Yes, that would probably be a good idea on both of those suggestions. Thank you for making breakfast. And you didn't burn the toast either. Sometimes our oven is unpredictable." Said Belle."

After they've eaten and the dishes are done, they get cleaned up, dressed, and head out the door for their walk down the hill to town.

When they step inside the store, Liza beelines it to the fabric department. She lingers over a rich looking, delicate, deep blue fabric made of the finest cotton sateen.

The Cumberlands of Caliente

Belle whispers to her daughter. "Liza, you need to pick something less expensive. This fabric is forty-nine cents a yard."

"Oh no. Sorry Mama. It's so pretty, but I didn't even look at the price. I just noticed how beautiful it was. I'll go find something else." Liza sighs dejectedly.

While Liza is wandering in the store and looking at other fabrics, Belle pays for the favored one and puts it in her purse. She will make something for Liza as a Christmas present.

Liza returns with two other fabrics that are in their price range. One is light purple with a diamond pattern on it and the other one is a deep coral color that has tiny leaves on it. "Here Mama, these are only twenty-nine cents a yard."

"That's great Liza. Those are pretty fabrics and they will make lovely dresses." Said Belle.

"Mama, I found a navy blue fabric with tiny swirls on it. Would that look good for a piano recital?" Asks Ella.

"Why don't you show me what you found?" Asks Belle.

Ella carries the bolt of fabric to the cutting table and spreads it out. "Yes, that would be beautiful made into a recital dress. Did you find any cloth for school dresses?"

"I found a bright red one that I really like and it's on sale for only fifteen cents a yard."

"You are a good shopper. If you can find another one for the same price, I can make you two school dresses. The navy blue fabric would be just for a recital dress and church."

"There is a dark red cloth that is the same price as the bright red one but it has a different design on it. I'll go get it." Ella comes back quickly with her other fabric choice.

"This one is beautiful too, Ella. And you're a good bargain hunter."

"Thank you Mama."

Mary shows her mother her first fabric choice. "Mama, what do you think of this heavier material? I really like the dark green. It's almost blue. I'm getting older and I want to look more sophisticated."

"It's a rich looking beautiful color. How much is it Mary?"

Mary sighs when she looks at the price. "It's thirty-nine cents a yard."

"That should be fine if you pick something a lot less expensive for the other dress that you want." Said Belle.

The Cumberlands of Caliente

"I will find something on sale. I saw a fabric in royal blue that is only nineteen cents a yard. It is a very fine looking fabric, and was originally forty-five cents a yard. I guess that nobody wanted it. But I like the color."

"Royal blue does look good on you." Said Belle.

"Even though the teacher hasn't taught us a lot yet, I would like to try sewing one of my dresses. Maybe you could help me with it." Said Mary.

"I can help you Mary, but hurry and get the blue fabric before somebody else does. It's a very good bargain and others might want it too. Plus we need to be going soon so that I can get some bread made for our supper tonight, and for us to have for our Sunday dinner tomorrow." Said Belle.

"We will help with supper Mama. Won't we?" Mary turns to Liza and Ella.

They take turns nodding their heads. "Yes, we will. I'll make us a pudding or a cobbler for dessert." Said Ella.

"I'll set the table." Said Liza.

After Liza finishes her Monday chores, doing the dusting and sweeping the kitchen floor, she reaches into one of the

Saturday shopping bags and carefully slides out her fabric and pattern. Soon she's spreading the fabric out on the table and is pinning the pattern pieces in place.

School will be starting in just two weeks and Liza wants to get her dresses made and ready to wear during the first week of school. She opens the drawer, gets out the scissors, and is ready to cut.

"Wait Liza." Belle checks Liza's pattern layout; and then helps her adjust the pattern pieces to get them pinned correctly to the fabric. With her mother's approval, she starts cutting carefully around the pattern pieces. Soon she will be sewing her first dress.

"Liza, move the pedal slowly so that your stitches will be straight."

"Okay Mama."

"And don't pull the fabric from behind. It will make it pucker and there will be skipped stitches."

"Okay, thanks for helping me."

"Maybe you would like to sew some on your other dress when you're done with this one." Asks Belle.

"I'd like that. The other one looks harder to sew. There are so many pattern pieces. Maybe you can help me with a lot of it. I'm not sure I can figure it out."

"I can help you with any of it. But I will need to work on your sisters' dresses too. Let me know when you need my help with the one that you're working on. I'm going to start cutting out Mary's and Ella's dresses on the dining room table." Said Belle.

Liza smiles at her mother. "Thanks Mama. I like sewing with you."

"You're welcome Liza."

Chapter nine

Seven months later

After Belle puts the last dish away from their evening meal, she heads to the front room to talk to Syd. He's reading the newspaper but looks up when he sees her enter. "Hi Belle. Come have a seat. You seem kind of tired."

"I think that it's just the gloomy March weather that we get before we have spring. We can't do a lot outside at this time of year because it's still too cold." Belle pauses for a minute and then comes back with a smile. "Syd, some of the families in the neighborhood are getting together for a potluck dinner and board games at the legion hall on Saturday evening. Do you want to go?" Asks Belle.

"What time is it on Saturday?"

"They're planning it for 6:00 to give people enough time to get their families together and drive over there."

"Since I'm off at 4:30, that should give us plenty of time to get there by six. What are you going to make Belle?"

"With the weather being cool, I've been in the mood for scalloped potatoes. I heard the Mr. Weatherly butchered and smoked a pig. And he will be bringing it. People are gearing their food around the ham that will be served. I'm also making some baked beans. Both of those dishes will go well with the ham."

"I always love your scalloped potatoes. It's the way that you season them, and then melt that special cheese on top that makes them so good."

"Why thank you Syd."

"I hope some of the ladies will be making pies and cakes."

"I'm sure Mrs. Stephens will be making her rich chocolate cake. It's always a hit at the potluck dinners. Mrs. Green will probably make some cream pies. And some of the other women will be bringing bread or rolls. Mrs. Canfield usually does and so does Miss Webber. We seem to get quite a variety of things to choose from at our potlucks."

The Cumberlands of Caliente

"I can't wait. It all sounds really good. Do we need to bring a board game?" Asks Syd.

"I'm planning on taking our Monopoly game that we got for Christmas. Our girls love it, and so do we. So I'm sure others will too."

Just before 6:00 o'clock on Saturday evening, Syd pulls their Studebaker into the parking lot of the legion hall. There are cars and trucks parked everywhere. Liza, Mary, Ella, and James eagerly open their doors and run inside. Soon Syd and Belle join them.

"It looks like we have more people than usual this evening. I see quite a few people from Company Row. I hope we're prepared because most of those railroad workers have big appetites." Laughs Syd.

"Yes they do. I've heard some of their womenfolk say that they are tired of being stuck inside at home during the winter. They want to get out and do something. And they really love coming to these potlucks." Said Belle.

"I think that our potlucks bring us closer together as a community. So it's good that we're getting out and mingling with one another."

The Cumberlands of Caliente

"I've been getting to know some of the railroad workers' wives. We have quite a bit in common."

Chapter ten

Blossoms have been on the trees for almost a month and are beginning to fall and blow away. With spring weather in their midst, Belle gets out her cleaning supplies to do deep cleaning on the main level as well as in the upstairs rooms of their home. School will be out soon and she knows her children can't wait for summer to begin. Caliente always has so many things for families to do in the summertime. There are picnics in the park, outdoor games, and swimming in the creek.

The Cumberland children are anticipating their favorite summer activity. It's the Fourth of July picnic and celebration. People from all over Lincoln County come to Caliente to enjoy it. With the approaching holiday that is coming up quickly, most of the planning has been done.

The Cumberlands of Caliente

The night before the event, Ella and Liza excitedly come in the front room of their home and plop down in front of their father to talk to him

"Papa, I can't wait until tomorrow when we have our July 4th picnic at the park. I like meeting new people. Do you know what kind of food and ice cream that they will have this year?" Asks Ella.

Syd puts down the book that he'd been reading to give his daughters his undivided attention. "I'm not sure. It's different every year. But there should be a variety of things to eat." Syd looks at one daughter and then the other. "I hope you helped your mother with the salads. We're taking three this time.

"I cooked the potatoes and I cut up the onions. My eyes didn't like the onions very much." Said Ella.

"Yes, they are pretty strong. You are a good help to your mother Ella."

"I cleaned up the mess Papa." Said Liza.

"That's very helpful too, Liza."

"People love your mother's potato salad as well as her macaroni salad. She makes the best salads ever." Said Syd.

The Cumberlands of Caliente

"She does. Will there be games at the park, Papa?" Asks Liza.

"There should be. They might have Red Rover, dodge ball, and some races." Said Syd.

"Papa, is it okay if Ella and I play kick the can before supper? Some of our friends are out there playing." Liza points outside.

"Yes, as long as you come back in time to help with Sunday supper."

"Thanks Papa. We will." Said Ella.

"Yes, thanks Papa." Said Liza.

When the Cumberland family enters the park late morning the next day, there are tables and tables laid out with desserts, salads, breads, and main dishes. They add their food to the mix. A barbeque pit has been set up to roast hot dogs and marshmallows. Families pull out their plates, cups, napkins, and utensils that they brought from home. They can't wait for the festivities to begin. Several ice cream makers are being cranked to put out several gallons of ice cream. Horseshoes have been set up as well as a fishing game with prizes for children.

The Cumberlands of Caliente

Soon the young and old are in line ready to get their fill of the bounty. A stream of salads has been set up on a table. There are several varieties of fresh fruit, potato, macaroni, and tossed salads. Pies and cakes of every variety are lined up on another table. A favorite among the adults is the caramel cream pie. A second fire pit has been set up to roast additional hot dogs for any latecomers and for the overflow crowd.

The children are first in line to get the ice cream. They pick their favorites among the peach, strawberry, and vanilla custard ice cream. They gorge themselves on the delicious frozen treat.

Ella walks sluggishly over to her mother and leans down. "Mama, I think that I'm going to be sick. I ate too much peach ice cream."

"Oh, Ella. Maybe you should lie in the shade next to the fence for a while. It might help you feel better. I'll roll up one of our blankets so that you can prop your head against it."

"Thanks Mama. I wanted to play Red Rover, but now I don't feel like it."

"If you rest for a time, maybe you'll feel better soon."

"I hope so." Ella relaxes and takes a short nap. Soon her sisters join their mother on a blanket near Ella.

"Dodge ball was fun, wasn't it Liza?" Asks Mary.

"It was. But I don't think James had much fun playing it. He got hit too many times with the ball." Said Liza.

"I'm glad that I got to run in a race too because I won a nickel." Said Mary.

"What are you going to buy with it?" Asks Liza.

"Probably a whole bag of candy. But I will share. I can get a whole lot of candy with just a nickel." Said Mary.

"I liked the hot dogs. And I ate two of them. They were so good with pickles, mustard, and catsup." Said Liza.

After playing three games of horseshoes, Syd leaves the others and comes back to join his family.

He whispers to Belle. "You should enter the soda cracker eating contest. I think you would win."

"You do?"

"Yes. It's getting ready to start in just a few minutes. Why don't you go to the entry table? I'm betting on you"

Belle laughs. "You might lose all your money." Soon she gets up and moves toward the table. Ten minutes later the contest begins. When the contestants finish eating their pile of crackers, they have to whistle. Syd was right. Belle beat all the other contestants by two minutes. She holds up her blue ribbon with one hand and then raises her other hand with a wave. She takes her ribbon back to Syd with her box of candy that was part of her winnings.

"Congratulations Belle. I knew you could do it."

Belle kisses Syd and sits down next to him.

"Mama, you were great." Said Mary.

"I'm going to enter that contest sometime." Said Liza.

"Will you share your candy?" Asks James.

"Of course James." Said Belle.

Ella raises herself up on one arm. "Mama, I'm glad you won." She whispers sluggishly as she flops back down.

A half hour later, Belle and Syd get up and shake the blankets that they'd been sitting on.

"It's getting dark. So it's time to go home." Said Syd.

"Ah, Papa, do we have to?" Asks Liza.

"They're shutting everything down anyway."

"Okay, Papa." Said Mary glumly.

The Cumberlands of Caliente

The next morning Liza is up early and having her breakfast alone ready to start her day. When her mother comes in the kitchen, Liza has a bright smile on her face while she's eating her oatmeal flecked with a dozen or more raisins.

"Morning Mama. My friends Edna and Dorothy are going down to the train station to watch the trains. May I go with them after I finish eating?" Asks Liza while averting her eyes from her mother.

"Liza, what are you going to do at the depot besides watch the trains?" Belle asks questioningly.

"When the freight train stops, we're going to hop on. And when the train leaves the station and gets to the top of the hill, we're going to jump off."

"Liza that is way too dangerous. Your father would take his razor strap to you if he found out you were doing that." Said Belle.

"Oh, it sounded like it would be fun. But I guess I could get hurt."

"Yes you could. Now, if you want to do something really fun, why don't you draw some pretty blouses and skirts, color them in with your pencils, and then show them to me. I think that I might have a few more colored pencils that you could borrow."

"Yes, that does sound better. And I really love to draw and design clothes. I wish I could draw better." Said Liza.

"Maybe Mary would show you. She's good at drawing."

"I'll ask her. But she always seems so busy with her art or reading."

"I'm sure she wouldn't mind helping you. She's a good sister."

"She is. I'll go talk to her when I finish my breakfast."

"That's much better than jumping off of freight trains." Said Belle.

Liza devours the rest of her oatmeal, then jumps up, and goes looking for her older sister.

Chapter eleven

After starting dinner preparations and opening the window to cool down the kitchen, Belle quietly steps in the parlor to listen to Ella's piano playing. When Ella hears her mother's approaching footsteps, she turns around and smiles.

"Mama, Miss Frye thinks I'm good enough to go to Las Vegas again this summer and take a more advanced piano class."

"She did come over and speak with your father and me. You were already in your bedroom when she came."

"Does that mean that I get to go?"

"We are still trying to decide if we can afford it. I know that it will only be for a month this time. But Miss Frye didn't think that there would be any scholarships."

"Oh, I didn't know that. We can't afford a lot of things right now. I understand." Ella says sadly.

"I will talk to your father again tonight."

The Cumberlands of Caliente

"Really?"

"Yes. We'll need to make a decision soon whether we can we can make it work or not because the summer music program is coming up soon."

Unbeknown to Ella, another piece of fine furniture has been sold. The possibility has become a reality for Ella to go to Las Vegas again for summer music school.

Just two weeks after Ella returns from Las Vegas, the family starts preparing for another school year. Mary has had enough experience from taking sewing classes in school to make her own school dresses this year. With very little help, Liza has sewn most of hers. She again had chosen an intricate pattern and has needed help to finish the details on one of them. Belle works with Ella showing her the fine art of sewing. But she continues to sew Ella's dresses because her daughter's interests lie elsewhere.

After the first week of school is over, Mary rushes in the door after visiting her neighbor on her way home from her last class. She goes from room to room in their house searching for her mother. She finally finds her in the backyard hanging out laundry.

The Cumberlands of Caliente

"Mama, I'm glad I found you. Mrs. Stephens has more canvases that she said that I could have. She found them in her attic yesterday. May I help her by babysitting her children to pay for them? She said that I could just have them. But I want to help her out again. Is that okay?" Asks Mary.

"When would she want you to baby-sit?" Asks Belle.

"Just whenever I can. It doesn't matter." Said Mary.

"That's thoughtful of you to offer and it's fine with me. Maybe you could babysit sometimes in the evenings or Sunday afternoons so that she and her husband could do something together."

"That's a great idea. Would that be like a date for them? Do married people even go on dates?" Asks Mary.

"Yes, they do if they get a chance to do it." Answers Belle.

"How come you and Papa don't go on dates?" Asks Mary.

"Your father is tired a lot when he comes home from work."

"You could go on a Sunday picnic after church, couldn't you?"

The Cumberlands of Caliente

"Yes we could, that's a wonderful idea Mary. I'll ask your father about doing that. I would enjoy it. And I think that he would too."

The following Sunday, Belle has a delicious lunch waiting for her and Syd to have on a picnic after church is over. She prepared a roasting chicken and a potato salad the day before, and Mary made some chocolate cookies. Syd's favorite food to eat on a picnic is always Belle's potato salad. She made plenty so that their children could have some too.

Within an hour after they get home from church, the car is packed and ready to go with food, lemonade, and a blanket. They leave their children behind and head down the hill toward the canyon. After a short ride they find a quiet place to lie out their picnic lunch near a stream.

"I love Rainbow Canyon Syd." Belle says as she looks toward the trees and stream near them.

"I do too. And thanks Belle for making us this wonderful lunch. It's been a long time since just the two of us did something together."

The Cumberlands of Caliente

"It has. And you're welcome. A lot of it was Mary's idea. She volunteered to make the cookies. After we eat, would you like to go wading in the creek?"

"That would be soothing to my tired feet because I spend so much time standing at my job. But I think that I'm finally getting used to it."

Syd takes Belle's hand as they walk toward the water and step in. The cold water startles Belle and she jumps back. She looks at Syd, laughs, and thinks to herself. 'This has been a good day for them. Having time alone with her husband buoys her up.'

The Cumberlands of Caliente

Chapter twelve

As the school term draws to a close for the holidays, all the Cumberland children are busy with activities except Liza. She comes in the kitchen where her mother is working on a Christmas fruitcake. She plops down in a chair and puts her chin in her hands. Then she picks up a cloth and starts rubbing at an already clean spot.

"Mama, I need to talk to you about something."

"What is it Liza?"

"I'd like to take sewing in school starting with the January term. I want to be even better at it."

"I'm sure that you could sign up for a sewing class. The first thing that they teach you is how to make is a laundry bag and then maybe an apron."

"But I don't want to take a beginner's class. I already know how to make an apron, and a laundry bag is too easy. I want something more advanced."

"Maybe the teacher would let you make something else, like maybe a skirt."

"Yes, I'd like to make a skirt. Maybe I could make a Easter skirt." She looks up dreamily and motions with her hand. "I would put rows and rows of ribbon near the bottom of it, and I would have shiny buttons going down the front. Then I would put ruffles on the hem."

"Now, don't get ahead of yourself. We would still need to sign you up for the class and ask the teacher if you could make a skirt or maybe something else. Is there is an advanced class at your school?"

"I don't know. I just know that there are sewing classes at school."

"We will have to find out."

"Oh goody."

The Cumberlands of Caliente

When the students return to school in January after the Christmas break is over, Liza is accepted into an advanced sewing class. She is the youngest in her class. But with her previous experience sewing with her mother at home, she not only makes a detailed skirt, but also a ruffled blouse to go with it. She proudly wears her skirt and blouse to watch her sister Ella play at yet another piano recital in Pioche during the spring.

The Cumberlands of Caliente

Chapter thirteen

By autumn, the economy has shifted upward and Syd is given another promotion and a healthy raise at work. Snow has fallen earlier than usual this year in Caliente. The winter weather puts the family in the mood for the holidays much sooner.

The Christmas catalogs had come in the mail earlier in the day. So Belle sequestered herself in her room to go through them. With a smile on her face, she chose several items that she knows her family will like and would want for Christmas. Then she tears out the form in the middle of the catalog, fills it out with her name, address, and the catalog numbers for the chosen items, ready to get presents ordered early for her family. Sometimes items are out of stock way too soon. She staples her check to the form, sticks it in the envelope, licks the envelope shut, and places a stamp in the upper front corner. She will have to remember to take it to the post office when she goes to get their mail tomorrow.

Mary has gotten an early start on a project for her parents for Christmas. Several evenings in a row she hid in the attic, away from the others, to work on her present.

Ella is stumped. What can she do to make Christmas special for her parents? Then a thought strikes her late one afternoon.

Liza found out that her sisters have been working on projects to make something for their parents for Christmas. But what can she do? Her talents are limited. She has an idea for her father, but what can she do for her mother. She will ask Mary for ideas and for some help.

After an especially busy Saturday, Belle shoves her arms into the sleeves of her winter coat and walks out the back door toward her husband.

The Cumberlands of Caliente

When Belle steps onto their back porch, Syd quits whistling, looks up and then back down while continuing to sharpen his razor. "Hi Belle."

"Hi."

It's three weeks before Christmas and Belle needs to talk to him about the upcoming holiday. "Syd, do you suppose that we could take the family to get a Christmas tree next weekend? I know it's early, but the kids have been asking. They are especially excited for Christmas this year for some reason."

Syd stops what he's doing to give her his full attention. "I could ask about leaving work a little early on Saturday. It would be fun to drive out of town a ways so that we could have more trees to choose from. I'll see what I can do about work. I'll let you know as soon as I find out."

"And, if you can get off early, I'll let the girls and James know about going tree hunting. I hope you can work it into your schedule. The children would love it."

"Mary, Ella, Liza, James, time to get up. We're going to get a Christmas tree today." Calls out Belle.

The Cumberlands of Caliente

"I thought that Papa had to work on Saturdays." Exclaims Mary.

"He just found out late last night that he could get today off. He worked late every night during the week. So his boss said that he could have this Saturday off."

"Mama, do you think that we could find some pine nuts too?" Asks Liza.

"Maybe, if your father knows where to look for some. They aren't always that easy to find. You have to find just the right kind of pine trees. Hurry up and get dressed. I made biscuits and gravy for breakfast. And I don't want the food to get cold."

All three girls jump out of their beds and run to grab some clothes from their chests of drawers. They paw through their drawers, flinging clothes aside looking for the right things to wear when spending time outdoors in the snow.

James is already out of bed in his room. He hurriedly gets dressed, and ready to go. When he comes downstairs, the buttons on his shirt aren't quite lined up.

After they've eaten their hearty breakfast and cleaned up the dishes, the family piles into their Studebaker. They head west out of town toward open land.

The Cumberlands of Caliente

"Papa, how far do we need to go to get a Christmas tree?" Asks Ella.

"Just a few more miles Ella."

Soon Syd pulls the car off the highway, turns down a dirt road, and drives a little farther. He stops the car and turns off the engine when he sees a copse of evergreen trees. The children immediately jump out and start running toward the trees. Syd lifts his axe out of the trunk and carries it with him toward a grouping of trees that are the right height for their home.

"Whose turn is it this year to choose a tree?" Asks Syd.

"I think that it's James turn." Said Belle.

The girls have resigned looks on their faces and sigh heavily. They sit on a fallen log and look at the various trees in front of them.

"James, which one do you want?" Asks Syd.

With a smile on his face, James points to one that he likes in the distance. "I want that one Papa." The one that James points out is several feet higher than their ceiling and wider than the largest room in their house.

"That is very nice tree, son, but it too big and too wide for our parlor."

"Oh. How about that one Papa?" James points to a smaller tree close by.

"You picked a fine tree James. Now everybody get back while I chop it down." The girls get up, from their log, and move far away from the tree that James had chosen. After a few chops, the tree falls to the ground.

"Timber." Yells James.

"Bombs away." Yells Liza. "Now, can we hunt for some pine nuts Papa?"

"Yes we can." Syd puts his hand on Liza's shoulder and points. "See that tree over there with all those pinecones on it."

"Yes."

"Those will probably have some pine nuts inside."

"Really?" Asks Liza.

"I believe so. I'll pull one off and check." Syd walks toward the evergreen and pulls off a cone to inspect it for pine nuts. "This one has some."

"Yeah."

"Liza, if I stand on my tiptoes I can yank some pinecones off of those higher branches for you." Offers Mary.

The Cumberlands of Caliente

"Thanks. I'll pull some off of the lower branches. Then we'll have a really big pile." Said Liza.

"I'll go get the buckets." Mary heads to the car and lifts some buckets out of the trunk to load their bounty of cones that they'll be pulling off the trees. Liza, Ella, and James have already piled a dozen or more pinecones on the ground by the time that Mary gets back.

Liza picks one up off the ground, pulls out some nuts, and starts to chew. "Mama, these pine nuts must be bad. They taste awful." She spits out what's left of the pieces that were in her mouth.

"You probably just like them better roasted. That's how we usually eat them." Said Belle.

"Oh, yeah. I do. I'll try to remember that next year if we go hunting for some." Liza says as she wipes out her mouth.

"Kids, we have our tree and plenty of pinecones. Now if everybody wants to get back in the car, we'll head home. Do you want to do something really fun when we get there?"

"What Papa?" Asks Liza.

"Yes Papa, what is it?" Asks James.

The Cumberlands of Caliente

"We could get out our pans and sleds and slide down Denton Hill." Yells Syd.

"Really?" Asks Mary.

"Oh goody." Says Ella.

"Papa, will you slide with us?" Asks James.

"Oh, maybe once or twice."

After Syd ties the tree to the top of the car, and they load the buckets of pinecones in the trunk, they head back to Caliente. The roads have been cleared, so the ride back goes quickly.

Soon Syd is pulling their sleds and pans out of their storage shed for their afternoon activity. By 5:00, all rosy-cheeked children enter the house and are ready for a hot supper.

Belle yells to her children when they enter. "Leave your boots on the porch. I don't want you tracking in snow and mud."

'Yes Mama' is heard from all four children.

"Supper should be ready in about half an hour. Liza, after you put your coat away, will you set the table?" Asks Belle.

"Yes, Mama. I'll hurry and do it. I'm hungry and I can't wait to have some of those roasted pine nuts sitting on the table."

"Thank you Liza. Don't eat too many pine nuts before supper though."

When Christmas morning comes, Mary, Ella, Liza, and James can't wait to give their parents the presents that they'd created. This year is really special for all three girls and James. They've worked very hard to have something unique for their parents for Christmas.

"Girls, James, your breakfast is ready." All four children lumber down the stairs and head to the kitchen. Laid out on the table are several oranges. Thick slices of bacon are kept warm on a hot plate. Hot cranberry muffins are set out in a basket. Cocoa is being kept warm on the stove. Soon freshly scrambled eggs complete their feast. Syd blesses the food and they dig in.

"Mama, I love these muffins. Will you make them again sometime?" Asks James.

"When I can get cranberries, I'll do it. Sometimes they're not available in the store."

"I hope you can get some more cranberries. I really like them." James says as he bites into his third one.

"Thanks for making us this wonderful breakfast." Said Syd.

"Yes, Mama. This is so good." Said Liza.

"Thanks for getting up so early to do it." Replies Mary.

"Yes, thank you Mama. I especially liked the bacon." Said Ella as she reaches across the table to grab another piece.

"When everyone is through eating, let's head to the parlor. We'll do the cleanup later. Okay Belle?" Smiles Syd.

"That's fine Syd. Our children can't wait to get to their presents.

Mary, Ella, and Liza hurriedly finish forking the food in their mouths. Then they run to their bedroom closet to get the presents for their parents. They come down the stairs just as fast as they went up and head to the parlor where their parents are waiting for them.

Mary speaks first. "Mama, Papa. Each of us made something special for you for Christmas. We helped James make something too. Here is mine that is for both of you." Mary hands her mother a large, brown, paper wrapped, package tied together with colored string.

Belle carefully unties the string, pulls the paper away, and shows Syd. They both have tears in their eyes when they view it.

"Mary, how were able to make such a beautiful painting of your father and me?" Asks Belle.

The Cumberlands of Caliente

"I pulled an old picture out of a photo album, kept looking at you during mealtime, and then kept the memories with me while I painted."

"If it's okay with your mother, we will hang it right here in our parlor." Asks Syd.

"I have something for you too." Said Liza. She hands over a knitted scarf to her father and a new handkerchief to her mother.

"Why thank you Liza. This will keep my neck warm when I need to wear my winter coat. It's soft too and not scratchy like some scarves are." Said Syd.

"Liza, how were you able to get me a hanky?" Asks Belle.

"Miss Frye needed cleaning done. So I earned money by doing it." Said Liza.

"Thank you, Liza."

"My present is a little different. You have to listen to it." Ella walks over to the piano, sits down, and leans a sheet of paper against the music holder. "I composed this song just for you, Mama and Papa. It's called **Christmas Song**. My really good school friend Cambria wrote the words. And I wrote the music."

"Cambria is an unusual name." Said Belle.

The Cumberlands of Caliente

"It's Welsh. She told me that one time. She is very smart and knew how to write really good words to go with my music."

Ella fingers fly over the piano keys using many quarter notes and eighth notes as she breaks into a beautiful melody.

♪♪

At Christmas me and my family

Like to decorate our tree

We hang the ornaments we made

With our family all day we stay

There's nowhere else I'd rather be

♪ ♪♪ ♪♪ ♪♪ ♪

There's nowhere else I'd rather be[7]

Ella carries the word **be** out a long time on the piano keys.

"That was so beautiful Ella. I hope you wrote down the words and notes." Said Belle.

"Cambria wrote the words on a piece of paper for me, but I haven't written down the music yet."

"I loved your piece." Said Syd.

"Thank you Mama and Papa."

"I have something for you too." Said James. "But it's not much."

---

[7] Words to **Christmas Song** – by Cambria L. Park

"I'm sure we will both love what you're giving us." Said Belle.

"I'll go get it." James leaves the room and comes back quickly with his hands loaded down. "Here. I made a Christmas wreath from the left over pinecones that we had after we dug out the pine nuts. I didn't want to throw all those nice pinecones away."

"You did a very nice job, son." Said Syd.

"My sisters helped me. Maybe we can hang it on the door. Mary and Liza found the pretty ribbons for the bow."

"I will get my hammer and a nail and hang it up when we're through opening our presents."

"You children don't know how special you made this Christmas for your father and me. You put your hearts and souls into making these wonderful Christmas gifts. Thank you." Said Belle.

"Yes, thank you children very much. No one could ask for better or more thoughtful children." Said Syd.

"Now open up all of your presents." Said Belle.

"YEAH!"

The Cumberlands of Caliente

All four children run to the present stash that is under the tree, and start tearing away at the paper covering the packages.

When school starts up again in January, some of Mary's friends are talking to her about what they did for New Year's Eve. Some of them had dates or went to parties.

"What did you do for New Year's Eve Mary?" Asks her older friend Eva.

"I wanted to earn some extra money by doing babysitting. But I spent my whole New Year's Eve doing it and all I got was a quarter." Complains Mary.

"That's all that they paid you?" Asks Eva.

"Yes. I'm never babysitting for that family again. Maybe I can find another type of job to earn money. I need to start saving if I want to go to art school."

"You are such a good artist. I hope you can go further with your education." Said Ida.

"Thank you Ida."

Chapter fourteen

The seasons have changed twice for the Cumberland family since Syd's job promotion. Mary is in her senior year in high school, and will be graduating with honors. Ella is in high school too. And Liza will be entering the next year. James is trailing not too far behind them.

Mary's talent in painting is celebrated by having some of her paintings on display in the downtown public offices, hotel, and the train depot in Caliente. A few of them are shown as far away as Las Vegas.

Part of her summers, Ella continues her piano lessons in Las Vegas at the same music school where she'd been before. She hopes to pursue her dream of getting a bachelor's of music degree. And then using that education to go further.

The Cumberlands of Caliente

With the help of her sister Mary, Liza is learning to draw much better. She is putting her clothing design ideas on paper so that she can turn them into actual articles of clothing someday.

The most studious one is James. He excels in history, science, and math. Someday he would like to start his own business. He has a head for business and has spoken with his father many times about pursuing that dream. Syd is hoping that James would one day want to be in business with him. Right now it's just a pipedream for Syd.

Chapter fifteen

Belle has had many dreams for her family for a long time. She wants all of her children to excel in school as well as in life. They have been good children growing up. And she wants the best for all of them.

After a long day of cleaning and washing the quilts on their beds, she finally gets their home ready for warmer days ahead. Summer is just around the corner. As she comes in her parlor to relax, do some embroidering, and have some quiet time to herself, she starts thinking about how much time has passed since she married Syd over twenty-two years ago. She can't believe that Ella is already a senior year in high school. Belle will relax some more before getting up to start dinner. Quickly she nods off and isn't disturbed until Mary walks in.

"Uh Mama."

The Cumberlands of Caliente

The voice jars her awake and her eyes flutter open. "Yes Mary."

"Oh, I'm sorry that I woke you up."

"That's okay. I need to get up soon anyway."

"Mama, do you know anything about scholarships?"

"I know a little about them. I could ask one of the counselors at the high school or you could."

"Do you suppose that Miss Frye might know? She knows about music scholarships."

"Why don't you ask her? Maybe you could stop by her home tomorrow evening after she's through teaching her piano lessons."

"I think I will. Thanks Mama."

"You're welcome."

Belle pulls herself up from her chair and heads to the kitchen to start on dinner preparations.

When Belle steps in the kitchen, Ella also wants to talk about school.

While she gets out the dinner dishes and helps her mother prepare the evening meal, she verbalizes her thoughts to her mother.

The Cumberlands of Caliente

"Can I talk to you and Papa tonight?"

"What is it Ella?" Asks Belle.

"I want to talk about school."

"Are you doing okay in school? Your grades are good.

"School is fine. I need to talk to you and Papa about what I want to do *after* I graduate."

"Oh. When your father gets home, I will let him know that you'd like to talk with both of us after dinner."

"Thanks Mama. I hope that Papa is in the mood for talking. Sometimes he isn't."

After dinner is over, Ella hurries through the clean up in the kitchen and puts the washed and dried dishes away. She's excited to talk to her parents about her plans down the road.

"Why don't we go sit in the parlor and talk Ella?" Asks Syd.

"Okay." Said Ella.

They take seats across from each other and Ella begins.

"Papa, Mama, I want to go to a music school in Las Vegas after I graduate from high school. Maybe I can find a job there to help pay for it. Miss Frye's sister, Grace, has let me stay with her before. Maybe I can do it longer this time. I like her and she's a really fun person. We get along great together."

"I know that you will be an adult by then. But we would still like to talk to Miss Frye and get her opinion about the different colleges in the area." Said Belle.

"We have been putting a little money aside for schooling during this past year. We could help you some." Said Syd.

"You could?"

"Yes, we've been planning on it." Said Belle.

"Thanks Mama and Papa."

Over their next Saturday morning breakfast, Mary excitedly tells her parents about the conversation she had the previous night with Ella's teacher.

"I spoke with Miss Frye last night. She knows about scholarships and art colleges. She said that there are good ones in California and New York. California is really close, but New York is just too far away. So I won't research any schools there." Said Mary.

The Cumberlands of Caliente

"My sister lives in Santa Monica. It might be possible for you to stay with her if you can get a scholarship at an art school that is somewhere near her. I'll write her and ask." Said Syd.

"Thanks Papa. I will get the names of the colleges in California, and the addresses if Miss Frye has them. If she doesn't, then the library or my school might have them."

After researching manuals in the library, her school, and talking to Miss Frye, Mary has the information in hand to request applications for schooling. After writing for, and receiving the forms in the mail, Mary sends the completed applications, along with photos of some of her paintings, to three different colleges that have good art programs. Two of them respond right away.

After opening up the letters from the schools, Mary hurriedly goes from room to room in their home looking for her mother. She finds her outside hanging up laundry.

"Mama, I got these letters in the mail from the colleges where I applied and sent pictures of my paintings. They are both offering me tuition. I am so excited. But I still need a place to stay."

The Cumberlands of Caliente

"Your father wrote his sister Marjorie. We'll have to see what she says. Hopefully we'll get something in the mail soon."

By the end of the week, a letter arrives in the mail addressed to Syd. The return address is in Santa Monica, California. Mary hands the letter to her father the minute he walks in the door from work. She nervously anticipates how her aunt will respond to her father's request.

"Okay Mary, let's see what's in the letter." Says Syd.

Syd tears off the end of the envelope, blows it open, and pulls out a letter. He reads it to himself, and then folds it back up.

"What did she say Papa?" Mary asks impatiently.

He smiles. "She would love to have you stay with her. And she said that you could stay for free if you would help her around the house. Your mother and I can help with some of your expenses such as art supplies or other miscellaneous things."

"Really, you think that this could happen for me? Since graduating from high school, you know that I've been saving my money from my job at the restaurant on Front Street. So I can buy a lot of my art supplies and my clothes. It looks like Ella and I will be going to college at the same time if everything works out for her too." Said Mary.

"Yes, it seems so." Smiles Belle.

"I think it's wonderful that my two oldest girls will be attending college." Said Syd.

The Cumberlands of Caliente

Chapter sixteen

James interests lie in political matters as wells as in business. His father usually answers a lot of his questions, but today Syd is not home. He is at work later than usual. So he turns to his mother with a quizzical look on his face when he walks into the family kitchen. He had been reading several sections of the weekly newspaper. But folds it up when he approaches her.

"Who's Hitler Mama?"

"He's a Nazi leader in Germany." Said Belle.

"He doesn't seem to be a very good person."

"No he's not." Belle says with a worried look on her face. "Why are you asking?"

"Some of my friends at school have been talking about him. They seem kind of worried." Said James.

"Hopefully what he's doing won't reach us."

"I hope not. There wasn't anything about him in our local newspaper. And I thought there would be." Said James.

"I would have thought so too."

James leaves the paper behind to climb the stairs to his room to do his homework.

Liza, who is also in the kitchen, seems unaffected by the conversation that was going on with her mother and James. She's concentrating on creating ornate designs with frosting on sugar cookies that are baked and cooled. She carefully sets them aside and turns to her mother.

"Mama, I'd like to go to art school like Mary. I want to be a better artist so that I can design clothes."

"For that kind of art, you would probably need to go to a clothing design school, maybe in California."

"I've seen pictures of California. I'd really like to live there. They have sunny beaches with beautiful water. And there is Hollywood too. The actresses in Hollywood and Beverly Hills wear all these elegant clothes." Says Liza dreamily.

"Why don't you go to the library and look up information about design schools? Or you could ask one of your teachers, they might know about those types of schools."

"Thank you Mama. I will talk to my art teacher and my sewing teacher. I'd like to go to one of those really good schools. My teachers would probably know about the best ones."

After a quiet Sunday evening, while the girls and James are all occupied with other things, Syd folds up his newspaper and looks in Belle's direction. She's been sitting in a chair doing some reading in their parlor. He loves looking at her. She is still beautiful after all these years, and after having four children.

"Belle, I'd like to talk to you for a few minutes."

"What is it Syd?" She sticks a bookmark in her book and lays it aside.

"I've been thinking about this for a while." He pauses for moment and then speaks rapidly. "I'd like to reopen up my company. I think that it will be successful again because of the changing economy." The air swishes out of Syd's mouth when he stops talking.

"Do you think that you will be able to make money if you do?" Belle asks worriedly.

The Cumberlands of Caliente

"People at the railyard have been asking for my financial advice. And the superintendent there would like me to do the accounting for the business. If everything would work out so that I could reopen, maybe James could come in part-time after school each day."

"I'm sure that he would love to do that. He's always had a head for numbers. Maybe Liza would too. She wants to earn money for design school." Said Belle.

"Before we decide if I should open the business again, I would put out feelers for any potential clients. I'd want to have several clients in place before I do it." Said Syd.

"That would be a good idea. It would be wonderful if you could reopen your business. I know how much you enjoyed it in the past and how much that it meant to you, your father, and grandfather." Said Belle.

One Saturday, late in the afternoon, Syd comes into his old place of business to look things over and do some work. He moves the desks and chairs that had been stored in the back of the building, and he begins to polish them. He knows that painting will need to be done too. The walls have turned into a dank, gloomy color over the years. Dust mites have wandered over the bookshelves. When Syd starts searching through some old boxes, several important items are unearthed. He finds his typewriter and log sheets, as well as other sundry items. He will hire people to take care of the painting, do some of the cleanup that needs to be done, and move the filing cabinets back in place.

After planning for several months and using some of their savings, Syd reopens the doors to his business. He proudly places the Cumberland name back on the front of the building in downtown Caliente where it was before.

"Belle, I'm glad we decided that I should reopen my business. I have more clients than I can handle. I am not only giving financial advice and doing investments, but several businesses have hired me to do their accounting and their bookkeeping. James and Liza have been a great help too. But Liza will be graduating and leaving soon. What would you think about coming to work with me at the office?" Asks Syd.

"I could do it part-time."

"You would? I need someone to do *my* books."

"Since you are a jack of all trades, you would be even busier if we were in a city. I'm glad that we are in a small town. We still need to have family time and couple time together. And I'd be sure that we'd *make* time for that."

Chapter seventeen

Belle is patiently waiting at the front door to usher James outside, but he is in a tither trying to find his best shoes and his favorite tie. He had to settle for second best on the tie. His growth spurt has been enough recently to cause his pants to pull above his socks.

"Hurry up James. We don't want to be late for church." Said Belle.

"Okay Mama." James skids to a stop in the family's front room, and looks in the mirror while trying to tie his tie.

"You're are getting really handsome son." Said Belle.

James blushes. "Thanks Mama."

"Well, we'd better hurry out to the car. Liza is inside. And your father has been warming it up."

The Cumberlands of Caliente

An hour and a half later the family comes home to a cozy house and gets ready to have their Sunday dinner.

"That was a really good meeting today Belle." Syd says as he unwinds his scarf, takes it off, and hangs it over his coat in the closet.

"Yes it was. I'll ask Liza to set the table and slice some bread. The roast and potatoes should be done anytime." Belle says as she stares at the hall clock.

"I will be in the front room listening to my Sunday radio program. Just call me when dinner is ready." Says Syd.

Syd settles into his favorite chair, turns on the radio, and moves the dial to his program. The radio show gets interrupted after just a few minutes. All of a sudden Syd jumps up.

"Belle, Liza, James, come in the front room. There is a special report on the radio that all of you should hear."

The family tunes in to the report about Oahu being bombed by Japanese airplanes. The casualties are in the thousands. There is destruction everywhere in Pearl Harbor and around Honolulu.

"That's horrible. Why would the Japanese bomb Pearl Harbor?" Asks Belle.

The Cumberlands of Caliente

"I don't know. But we will probably have another world war. I thought that the last one was bad enough. I'm guessing that all the young men around here may be gone soon."

"Let's eat our dinner and have a special prayer for our soldiers and for those who lost their lives today." Said Belle.

The next day, December 8, 1941, FDR addresses the American people. He calls the attack on Oahu 'Infamous Treachery.'

That same night, the newspaper proclaims **'War is declared on Japan by the U.S.'**

The Cumberlands of Caliente

Chapter eighteen

One and half years later

Most of the Cumberland children are grown and out of their home, and making a life for themselves. James is the only one left behind. Mary, Ella, and Liza keep in touch with their parents, by letters and telephone calls on a regular basis.

"Syd, I'm glad all of our children are doing so well. I guess you read Mary's letter. Her fiancé is a fellow artist. When the war is over, they want to go to Paris and paint, but they want to be married first."

"That's a good idea. I haven't read her letter yet."

"It came in the mail today."

"What else did she say?"

"She wants to get married at the church in town, but they will be going back to Los Angeles after the ceremony."

"I wonder why he isn't in the war."

The Cumberlands of Caliente

"She told me when they first started dating that he was injured when he was young and it prevented him from being in military service."

"I didn't know that. I read Ella's letter yesterday. So our Ella will be playing at Carnegie Hall?" Said Syd.

"Yes, isn't that wonderful? I'd love to go hear her play." Said Belle.

"Maybe we can. They still have passenger trains in and out of Caliente."

"Oh, I hope that we can do that Syd. Ella would love our support." Said Belle.

During the next month, preparations are made for someone to take care of Syd's business for two weeks. Then tickets are purchased for their train trip to New York City to meet up with Ella.

Syd and Belle get a ride from their neighbor to the train station early on a Monday morning to start their cross-country trek.

After three days on the train, they arrive at Grand Central Station. Belle is in awe of New York City. She has never been this far east and neither has Syd. The sights and sounds of such a big city are new and different for them. Together with Ella, they see the Statue of Liberty, museums, and Radio City Music Hall.

The highlight of their trip will be Ella's performance at Carnegie Hall. She's anticipating it nervously because of the large crowd that will be there.

"Mama, Papa, I'm excited about tomorrow night, but I'm also nervous. I've never performed in front of so many people."

"Just concentrate on your music and you will be fine." Said Syd.

"Just picture in your mind that the audience is full of monkeys." Said Belle.

Ella laughs. "I'll do that. Then I won't be so nervous."

The next night after the crowd has thinned, Ella looks down from the stage at the empty chairs and sees her parents coming toward her.

"Ella, you were wonderful." Said Belle.

"We are so proud of you." Said Syd.

"Thank you Mama and Papa for coming here and seeing me play. It wouldn't have been the same without both of you here." Syd and Belle see tears rolling down Ella's cheeks.

The Cumberlands of Caliente

"We loved coming to hear you play and spending time with you in New York City. We had a great time." Said Belle.

"Yes. We enjoyed all of it. Tonight, you couldn't have made us prouder." Said Syd.

Chapter nineteen

After having rain earlier in the day, the sun is out and the sky has changed from gray to blue. Belle decides it's a good time to walk to the post office to get their mail. She likes the rain, but sometimes it makes the road down their hill slippery. She says 'hi' to two of her neighbors on her way there. When she walks inside the post office, she opens their mailbox, thumbs through their mail, and then pulls out an envelope from Mary. She tears it open with her finger and starts to read while walking back home. When she walks inside their house, she stuffs the letter back in the envelope and lays it on the end table by the front door. She'll show it to Syd when he gets home if he doesn't notice it laying there first. She knows the wait won't be long. Just then, Syd walks in the door.

"Hi Syd, we got another letter from Mary today. She wants a June wedding."

The Cumberlands of Caliente

"What day?" Syd asks as he sits down in his favorite chair.

"She didn't say. But we need to find out so that we can help her with her plans."

"We certainly do. I need to know the date so I can close the business for a couple of days."

"I hope that her next letter tells us. I don't think that she has a telephone where she is staying. She usually just goes to a phone booth if she wants to call us."

"So we can't call her?"

"No."

"Now when does Liza graduate from design school, I can't remember?" Asks Syd.

"It will either be next spring or late summer. She might be taking some additional classes because she'd like to have her clothing shown in catalogs some day."

"I'd like to see that happen some day too. She is very tenacious about her plans. When James graduates from high school next year, he wants to go to college for a degree in accounting, or go even further and get a degree in law. I think that he is leaning more toward accounting, but who knows? He was talking to me about it when he came in to help me at work yesterday." Said Syd.

"Did you know that Liza has a boyfriend? I read her letter and set it aside, but then I forgot to give it to you. Her boyfriend wants to be an architect. So there are two letters for you to catch up on." Said Belle.

"Really?"

"Yes. Liza's boyfriend's name is Sam and he is going to a school close to hers. She met him one time at a church function." Said Belle.

"I'm glad that Liza is finding time for church."

"She told me that it's important to her. I'll bet they're getting serious if she is telling us about him."

"I'm thinking the same thing Belle."

"Liza also included some pictures in her letter. Let me grab it." Belle turns around and picks up the letter off of the end table. "This is what she said. 'Mama, I tore these pictures out of the Montgomery Ward catalog. I think these dresses would be really beautiful on you.'

Belle hands the pictures over for Syd to see. "Belle, those dresses would look really nice on you."

"Why, thank you dear."

8

---

[8] Spring and Summer Montgomery Ward - catalog

"Syd, she goes on to say. 'I would like these dresses for me. Maybe I could make ones that are similar. I like the cut and the style.'**9**

"That's our Liza. She always has those creative ideas flowing."

---

[9] Spring and Summer 1943 Montgomery Ward - catalog

Chapter twenty

After having an early Saturday dinner alone with Belle, Syd picks up his dishes and takes them to the kitchen. He does the cleanup with Belle to help her out and to spend time with her.

Afterwards, he leaves the room to sit in a chair in the parlor and read the newspaper. He puts the paper down when Belle enters several minutes later.

"Belle, did you hear that the railroad is changing from steam to diesel engines? And I heard that they are going to be moving the operations to Las Vegas."

"No, I didn't know about that. It will probably affect a lot of jobs."

"I'm sure that it will. I'm glad that I have my own company again. Most of my work comes from the local businesses. So hopefully that won't affect my business. But I am

The Cumberlands of Caliente

still concerned about those railroad workers. Maybe some of the workers will transfer. The railroad will need workers in Las Vegas with the operations being relocated."

"I hope things will be okay for those workers. I have become friends with some of their wives."

Belle looks around the parlor as if looking for something. "Uh Syd, I can't remember what time that Mary and Edward's train will be here. I'd better go find her letter."

"They are supposed to be on the 9:05 tonight. I know that we've never met Edward, but I'm sure that Mary picked a good one. She has good sense like that."

"I'm sure he's a wonderful man or Mary wouldn't be with him. How about we leave at 8:30? That way we could walk around the depot for a while and get a cup of cocoa in the hotel before their train arrives. I love the Spanish architecture of the building. It's a beautiful tribute to the City of Caliente." Said Belle.

The Cumberlands of Caliente

Epilogue

All of the Cumberland family, as well as many relatives, have gathered in Caliente to attend the wedding of Syd's and Belle's oldest daughter, Mary.

Syd's sister Marjorie arrived by train from Los Angeles the day before. Belle's sisters, Lucile, Nellie, Edna, and Mame had come two days earlier to help with the food for the wedding.

Because of her artistic abilities in making clothing, Liza designed Mary's wedding dress. Belle ordered the finest silk from Europe for the gown along with some luxurious embellishments. White pearl buttons line up the back of the dress and are on the sleeves as well. The veil is made out of fine netting with the edges trimmed in French lace. Belle, Mary, and Liza used their combined creative talents to sew the beautiful dress. Ella will be using her talents by playing classical music on the piano for the wedding and the reception.

"Syd, doesn't our Mary make a beautiful bride?" Asks Belle.

"She does. She reminds me of you when we got married. She has your dark beautiful eyes and hair. Would you like to dance some more Belle?"

"Yes, thanks Syd. Lead the way."

"Mary's wedding reminds me of our wedding day. I can't believe that it has been twenty-seven years since that day. Where did the time go?"

Syd hums softly to Belle as he spins her around and they continue dancing to the soft music that is being played at the wedding reception.

Printed in Great Britain
by Amazon